VAMPIRE'S IRE

A Ruby True Magical Mystery 3

NOVA NELSON

ISBN-13: 978-1-7367289-2-5

Cover Design © FFS Media LLC

Cover design by Molly Burton at cozycoverdesigns.com

Vampire's Ire / Nova Nelson -- 2nd ed.

Previously published as *Vampire's Ire, True & Bloom* 3

www.eastwindwitches.com

CONTENTS

VAMPIRE'S IRE

A Ruby True Magical Mystery 3

NOVA NELSON

Chapter One

Ruby True inhaled the delicious air of the tearoom. There was no finer way to get an early start on the day. The first scent that greeted her was the delicate flavor of bergamot and citrus. Following closely behind it, in the way a watchful parent might as their baby takes its first steps into toddlerhood, came the warm, nourishing scent of fresh baked pastry.

She closed her eyes where she sat at her favorite table in the back of A New Leaf, brought her library book up to her nose, and turned the page, inhaling the smell of old paper, adding it to the fragrant symphony of this space, her favorite place to spend her days outside of the attached cottage she called home.

If Ruby were to keep her eyes closed, she could very well pretend she was back in the world she grew up in, where no one flew around on brooms, werebears and elves were merely fodder for fairytales, and she didn't have any psychic powers to speak of.

Of course, that illusion would be dashed the second

she opened her eyes again and found herself in the cozy yet deadly town of Eastwind. Despite having lived here for eighteen years now, she could easily slip back into the mindset of her younger self, back before she died in her old world and wound up here instead of in the afterlife.

She opened her eyes. A baby faun, cradled on its mother's lap a table over, stared at her. The kid's furry legs kicked, one of its hooves knocking against the table leg, while the mother gabbed in low tones to the friend next to her. Ruby made a silly face at the kid and waved, but the baby showed no sign of comprehension, just kept staring.

Ah, well, babies were a little boring anyhow.

She brought her hot tea to her lips—not Earl Grey, since such a thing didn't strictly exist in Eastwind, but a very close version of it—and returned her attention to today's library book. *The Werewolf Heir's Sordid Affair* wasn't going to read itself, and there was no point letting one of her few days off between clients go to waste.

But as she turned her attention back to the page, trying to locate the paragraph where she'd left off (something about the stunning and tragically tortured hero's deep desire to find a witch who might free him from his father's curse), the door to A New Leaf opened and, with a burst of the bitter November air swirling its way inside the cozy space, in stepped a large figure. Ruby didn't even have to look up to know who was there. She could sense his presence. Not in any sort of psychic way, but about as well as anyone could sense the sudden arrival of a man they'd been pining for in the lonely hours of the night.

She snuck a peek, hoping Zax Banderfield wouldn't

notice her looking. It was clear he hadn't. Much to Ruby's dismay, the werebear's attention was fully focused on the woman who had just entered the tearoom ahead of him.

It was obvious in an instant that the pair had arrived together, and Ruby didn't kid herself that they were here on any sort of official business. Zax, all six-foot-yes-please of him, was the leader of the werebear sleuth that lived up on Fluke Mountain, and this woman, with her tall, slender body and silky-smooth hair, was no werebear. Nope, no official sleuth business happening there.

Perhaps it's High Council business, Ruby's voice of hope whispered to her. *Perhaps that's why he's spending time with a gorgeous, wrinkle-free elf like her.*

It wasn't outside of the realm of possibility. After all, some diplomatic relations between species must be attended to by the leaders of each group if Eastwind was to maintain a gentle peace between such disparate peoples. The elves had a representative on the High Council, and although Ruby knew it wasn't this particular one, perhaps this beautiful woman was simply a proxy of some sort, conducting business on behalf of Diarmuid Astrid. Perhaps the elf chieftain was tied up elsewhere and had assigned her to conduct business with the werebears in the meantime.

But then Zax leaned down to whisper something to his elven companion, who giggled and smacked him playfully on his thickly muscled arm, and Ruby could pretend no longer.

What did she expect anyway? It wasn't as if Zax hadn't given a romance with Ruby its fair shot. It was nobody's fault but her own that it was the elf and not she who had entered alongside the handsome werebear. He'd certainly tried to make it work just as much as she had. But she had put her work first, time and time again.

To be fair, so had he. And that was where the impasse had arisen.

Perhaps this elf didn't work. It was entirely possible, given the wealth that existed in the elven community, hidden up there in their own invisible neighborhood of Tearnanock Estates, separate from the usual toil of the town. Perhaps Zax had found himself a partner who was more willing to accommodate his schedule.

And is prettier and taller and younger than me.

She reeled in her inner critic. The *younger* part couldn't be verified, anyway. Elves didn't age the same way as witches, like Ruby, did. But this woman certainly *looked* younger than Ruby's forty-seven years.

"If that's all that matters to Zax, he never deserved you in the first place." The voice that had spoken was one only Ruby could hear, and it came from her shaggy hellhound familiar, whom she'd *thought* was dead to the world on his large dog bed in the corner of the tearoom. But perhaps her distress had roused ol' Clifford. In moments of strong emotion, her connection to her familiar could be especially strong without her realizing it.

Through their telepathic connection, Ruby replied, *"Thank you, Cliff. But I'm fine. Really."*

And yet, she couldn't stop staring at the flirtatious pair as they dallied by the front door, making quite the show of their chemistry.

Why had Zax come here? He knew this was her spot. Was it to taunt her?

No, Zax isn't like that. They were probably just in the

Emporium and needed a pick-me-up to start their day. This is the obvious place to come for that.

The elf and werebear made for the counter, behind which stood the elderly shop owner, Harley Hardtimes. The West Wind witch wore a hard expression as the new customers approached, and Ruby watched closely as Zax continued further into the tearoom with a puzzled caution. Then something seemed to click in the werebear's expression, and he indulged a quick scan of the shop, his eyes landing almost immediately upon Ruby. She was clearly what he'd been searching for, and he'd found her.

Dawning comprehension and a shade of guilt colored his face, and after muttering something to his elven friend, the two of them turned and left the tearoom without ordering.

Harley caught Ruby's eye, sighing tiredly before scurrying around to prepare what Ruby assumed would be a sympathy offering for her. She didn't especially like or need sympathy, but she would never turn down one of Harley's baked goods for any reason... so long as it didn't fail Clifford's poison sniff test. And even if it did, her rejection of it depended heavily on what *kind* of offering. She might still eat, say, one of Harley's lemon poppy seed muffins, regardless of poisoning. There were worse last meals, no doubt.

She briefly considered closing her eyes and tapping into her gift of Insight. It was an easy enough way to well and truly intrude on Zax's relationship with the elf, to learn what precisely was taking place between them. But she quickly decided against it. More knowledge in this situation could only hurt her further.

So instead, she turned back to her book. A little escapism sounded nice, and if that escapism included a broody and lonesome heir whose cold exterior could only be penetrated by a plucky and headstrong witch, even better.

Before she could locate the last sentence she'd read, however, a familiar voice from a table next to hers interrupted. "I happen to know Filaemenia Astrid is *far* too old for him anyway."

The voice had the slightest hint of an accent that Ruby, in her former life, might have assumed to be Eastern European. She didn't know what the equivalent was in Eastwind, what realm connected to this one (or connected to one connected to this one) might have caused Count Sebastian Malavic's voice to sound just such. It was irrelevant to her now, though. He was butting in. As usual.

Ruby turned in her seat toward the count. "Why are you even here? I didn't think you got up this early, and you don't drink tea."

The vampire smirked at her and raised a delicate cup to his lips. "You're right. I prefer a latte."

"And I would prefer it *a latte* if you'd keep your pale nose out of my business."

Malavic shrugged, unaffected. "I'm only trying to help. I remember when Filaemenia was born. If my memory serves, she's two hundred and twenty-one." He paused. "I suppose that means she has exactly two hundred years on you."

"Don't you try to flatter me, Malavic." But a small grin slipped onto her lips anyway. Ah, to be twenty-one again...

Malavic grabbed his latte and his copy of the *Eastwind Watch* and invited himself to the empty seat at her table. Ruby wanted to tell him to scram, but she found she couldn't muster the energy.

"Fine. I won't flatter you," he said. "Instead, I'll say Filaemenia is as empty-headed as anyone I've ever met. Her father sits on the High Council, you know. She's technically the eldest of his fifty-six children and should thereby follow him in that position when he decides to step down, but Diarmuid Astrid has made it clear to the rest of us that he has no plans for it. The poor woman can't even do multiplication, last I heard."

Ruby was feeling better already, but she tried not to let it show. "Well, math can be hard."

"She struggles with *single digit* multiplication, my dear death witch. Even subtraction is tricky for her. The only time I've ever seen her slum it in Sheehan's Pub, she left an entire silver for a pint of O'Shea's Blond."

"An entire silver? She would deserve change back on a copper! And what's she doing drinking O'Shea's Blond anyway?" Ruby caught herself and tried to glare at the vampire. The wan attempt only evoked another grin from him. "Okay, fine," Ruby conceded, "you've lifted my spirits, but *not* by appealing to my better nature."

"I wouldn't dare appeal to something so vile as *that*."

Harley Hardtimes appeared with a plated fruit and custard tart, which he set on the table in front of Ruby with a smile. As she nodded her thanks for the sympathy sweet, Malavic said, "Go ahead and add her bill to mine."

"This one's on me," Harley said, nodding at the tart.

"That's wonderful of you. I'll take the rest of her order on my check."

When Harley shrugged and departed, Malavic turned back to Ruby. "See? You still have all sorts of men attending to your needs without that big, ursine oaf sniffing around. Good riddance."

Ruby popped a blueberry from the top of the tart into her mouth. She didn't usually start her day with this much sugar, but perhaps she ought to. "I know what you're trying to do here, Malavic, and it's not going to work."

He smirked. "It did once."

Ruby felt her cheeks flush. It was true. His tactics had worked on her before, and it *had* been a nice bit of indulgence...

She pulled her mind back to the present. "*Once*. One time. But never again. I've learned your tactics, Sebastian. You stalk like the predator you are until you spot a moment of weakness, and then you swoop in."

"Yes, we vampires do love a good *swoop*. But I think you're mistaking my simple kindness for something less noble."

"I'm not mistaking anything. I know all about your kindness. So does all of Eastwind. It always comes at a price."

He sipped his latte slowly then said, "People gladly pay the price for things they crave. High-end brooms, powerful gemstones, anti-aging potions. They hand over the coins with a smile on their faces for the promise of something they desire on such a deep level."

She glowered at him. "You're no high-end broom, Malavic."

"You're right, I'm a much smoother ride."

Ruby's mouth fell open, and instead of chiding him

like she knew she should have, she did a very stereotypical thing for a witch.

She cackled.

Sebastian grabbed the fruit tart from her plate and brought it up to her lips for a nibble. He'd won this round, and he was gloating now.

She snatched the pastry from his hand and bit into it, trying with all her might not to moan at the sweet and tart flavors combining so sensually on her tongue. Now was *definitely* not the time or place for a show like that.

"What do you miss most about your old world?" Malavic asked as she savored the flakey puff pastry.

"My old world? Why do you ask?"

"There are just so few people who come to Eastwind from anyplace else. Most are locals and nothing else. At most, they've taken an overpriced vacation to Avalon, but they've never *lived* anywhere else. You have. So have I. I'm just curious what it is you miss the most."

"The food," she said without hesitation. "I'm sure it'll come as no shock to you that I frequently went against common wisdom and traveled the country solo as a young woman. That was frowned upon in those days. Women were meant to *stay put* and it was up to the men to roam. Very different from here, thankfully."

"But you roamed anyway?"

"I did. And when I did, I enjoyed the tastes of each new place. They were so unique. You could order much of the same cuisine elsewhere, but it always tasted so much better in the place where it belonged. Crab cakes in Chesapeake Bay, brisket in Texas... Ohh! And beignets with café au lait in New Orleans. And you could get this chocolate sauce to dip them in..."

The count's eyebrows rose. "New Orleans?"

"Yes, it was a wonderful place for a single woman like me to visit. Deliciously indulgent in every way. But the food—sweet baby jackalope—no one and I mean *no one* fries things like the Cajuns. They even make okra delicious." She pulled up short. "But look at me! Here I am with a delightful dessert right in front of me and I'm thinking about other treats. You've made me food cheat."

He leaned forward. "And if I'm not mistaken, I believe I've also made you feel better." He finished the last of his latte and stood. "Never fear, my dear Fifth Wind, I'll tempt you no further. Instead, I'll simply be a perfect gentleman and say my duty here is done since I succeeded in making you smile. Enjoy the rest of your tea and tart. I hope your day only gets better from here." He nodded congenially at Clifford, who growled at him. "Fair enough." And then Count Malavic grabbed his newspaper, dropped off more than enough coins at the counter for Harley, and departed, leaving Ruby in a confusing swirl of her own senses.

Chapter Two

109 years before the present

Sheriff Gabby Bloom hadn't had time to meditate in seventeen days, and it was leaving the angel a little agitated.

"Mr. Scandrick," she said, holding back her temper, fighting the more vengeful impulses of her nature as she addressed the belligerently drunk werewolf with as much courtesy as she could muster, "I'm going to ask you to put your shirt back on and stop using anti-witch language. Aiden Sheehan has already warned you once, and as I hear it, he was both clear and kind in the way he asked."

They stood under a starry sky and a full moon outside the town's most popular late-night spot, Sheehan's Pub, and Bloom tried not to think about how much she would have preferred to be inside with a cold beer instead of out here with this drunken fool. It was unreasonable to expect one woman, however talented and competent she might be, to enforce all the laws on her own, even in a town of this modest size. She needed help, especially so long as she was expected to respond to every intoxicated werewolf causing a scene outside of the Outskirts.

"It was a compliment!" Loren Scandrick declared, shouting the words so loudly the effort almost took his feet out from under him.

"Not all witches wear hats, Mr. Scandrick. Calling them 'a bunch of cackling coneskulls' is considered offensive."

"When I was young—"

"You're not anymore. You're not sober anymore either, so I think it's time to head home."

The front doors of the pub opened, and two tall figures stepped out.

"What's all this?" asked Count Sebastian Malavic, striding up. Behind him followed a cloaked figure with a scythe strapped to his back.

Bloom spared a short glance for both the vampire and the grim reaper before gluing her eyes back to the drunkard at hand. "Mr. Scandrick has had enough to drink for the night, that's all. I was just about to escort him home."

The grim reaper stepped forward. "He was being rather rude, Sheriff. I told him to stop, but he wouldn't listen." His voice was dry and cracked, like a hex bag of bones being shaken, but Bloom didn't find it altogether unpleasant. Perhaps some of that could be attributed to how much she liked the reaper.

"That's kind of you, Ted. I appreciate your trying."

"Least I can do, heh."

Loren Scandrick turned toward Ted, seeming to only

just realize the hooded figure was there, and his eyes crossed. "You think you're so tough, Death?"

Ted straightened, sending a ripple down his robes. "No, I really don't."

Bloom was done with this. Attempting to pick a fight with a reaper was not only beyond the pale, but also beyond the veil.

As Scandrick attempted to march toward Ted (he was on entirely the wrong trajectory, however, and was as likely to run into the side of the pub as he was the psychopomp), Sheriff Bloom summoned one of the few fun spells she had in her angelic arsenal.

Two glimmering strings of gold shot from her hands. The first hobbled the werewolf, causing him to go down. Once he'd used his hands to break the fall and ensure no major head trauma, the second string bound those at the wrist as well.

Count Malavic chuckled at the spectacle.

"Seems you need a time out, Mr. Scandrick," said Bloom. "Now, you have a choice. You can spend the night in a cell to sleep it off, or you can head back to your compound and sleep it off there."

"Get these things offa me!" he shouted.

"Oh, for Heaven's sake, will you shut up, man?" She shot another golden string at him, and this one clamped like a gag around his mouth.

She flicked her wrist and Loren Scandrick was lifted back into his feet facing her. He had to listen now. "I'm giving you a choice. A cell or your own bed?"

His response was muffled, so she vanished the gag. "Bed, please," he said.

She forced a smile. "That's better."

Ted stepped forward. "Would you like me to take him back? The Scandrick Compound is on my way back to the Deadwoods."

Bloom nodded. "I would be much obliged, Ted. I'll leave the cuffs on, and if he gives you any trouble, just use the blunt end of that scythe to subdue him." She gave Ted a quick wink that the werewolf missed, and the reaper responded with, "Heh. You got it, Sheriff."

Off the two of them went.

"That was one of the most enticing acts I've witnessed in a very long time," came the count's voice from behind her.

She turned tiredly toward him. "That was not my better nature shining through."

He strode forward out of the shadows and into the moonlight. "You should let *not your better nature* shine through more often, then. It's *delightful*."

She really must have been overtired and meditation-deprived, because when she looked at Malavic's half-grin in this moonlight, she found her usual disdain for the selfish vampire had lessened. "I'm just a little overworked, is all. Sure, I could manage the entire town on my own a century ago, but the population has grown, and with the insane incident reports the High Council requires me to file for every interaction..." She sighed. "Faith and feathers! This exchange with Loren Scandrick alone will take me an hour to write up, if I can even find that somewhere between the calls."

Malavic nodded. "Sounds like you need help."

"Ah, you're actually listening to what I'm saying? Color me shocked, Malavic. If I didn't know any better,

I'd think my moment of weakness might have brought out *your* better nature."

"I don't have a better nature. Not anymore. But if I did, I'm sure you'd be the one to suss it out." He stepped closer, meeting her gaze. "When you look into my eyes, you sense nothing. Isn't that correct?"

She could smell the rich scent of expensive wine on his breath now. "I can't summon my Judgment, if that's what you mean. I can't sense any guilt within you, but I know it's there all the same. It has to be."

His voice was hardly more than a whisper. "It doesn't have to be. Only those with a soul are obligated to carry that particular burden. You think I should feel guilt for the things I've done, but I do not."

"I don't believe it," she said. "I may not be able to judge your soul, but that doesn't mean you can't feel guilt for actions you know to be wrong."

His tilted his head to the side almost imperceptibly. "Are you so sure?"

"Yes, I am."

"How can you be?"

"Because I know you weren't always a vampire. Mortals may see you as that, because you've been a vampire for many of their lifetimes over. But I'm not a mortal. I don't view people with such short-sightedness. You were something else before you were turned, and that something else remains inside of you somewhere, even if I can't access it."

Was it just her imagination, or had his expression actually turned to stone? But then he raised his chin. "It's true. I was something before. But that man is dead. Well, undead." He stepped back and the cord of tension between them snapped. "If you need help," he said, his tone much more relaxed now, "you should have said something to the High Council."

"I have."

"Then you should have been louder about it."

Bloom struggled again against mounting frustration. "I've been plenty loud. You and the rest of the Council have just ignored me."

"Well, as the trusted treasurer, I do have quite a bit of say in budgetary matters, and if it's money you need to continue doing the stand-up job you are, then it's money you shall get. However, I don't love the notion that more money and less stress for you will likely result in fewer shows of force like the one I was treated to just now." He grinned shamelessly. "It's a whole new twist to *showing some restraint*, but you don't see me complaining."

Too tired to respond, Bloom simply rolled her eyes.

"I'll send an owl your way with an invitation to the next High Council meeting," Malavic concluded. "I hope you'll come plead your case for more robust funding. If you do, I'll make sure it happens."

She eyed him warily. "Thanks?"

"You're welcome. You do great work, Sheriff." He clapped a cool hand onto her shoulder. "We're lucky to have you."

With that, he turned and strolled off into the darkness, and Gabby Bloom, an avenging angel from Heaven, was left in a stunned state at having just received a genuine compliment from the most detestable man in Eastwind.

Chapter Three

Presently

Ruby True wasn't thinking at all about Zax Banderfield as she settled down into her reading chair by the fireplace after a light, early lunch. Instead, she was thinking about beignets. She hadn't thought about *those* in a very long time, but now she was considering whether it would be worth her effort to describe them to the town's baker, a gray-haired South Wind witch with deep wrinkles like folded dough, to see what he could come up with. It certainly *would* be nice to have one after so many years.

A knock at her cottage door interrupted her plotting.

Knock knock knock... knock knock.

Not a dark entity then. That was always a pleasant surprise. While most people in Eastwind knew better than to only knock on her door three times, there was an occasional ignoramus, and they were awarded with no answer from her. She'd learned her lesson the hard way when she'd first arrived in town that anything knocking thrice brought nothing but bad news.

The fact that whoever this was had knocked thrice, then a pause, and then twice more, led Ruby True to believe that someone might be messing with her. And the only person she knew who was brave enough to risk that (or rather, who was not only aware that Ruby was not the death bringer that most of the town thought she was, but also that a tongue lashing from her wasn't actually that bad) was Sheriff Gabby Bloom.

And sure enough, it was the angel who stood on Ruby's front step. "Am I under arrest?" Ruby asked. It was always good to get that out of the way first.

"Not this time."

Ruby shivered as the cold air hit her. It was colder than usual for late November, and the late-morning sun was doing little to warm up anything. Were she still in her old world, she might have been celebrating Thanksgiving this week, but Eastwinders had no such tradition. Fine by her. She would simply treat herself to a feast whenever she wanted, then! "Well, if you're not going to arrest me, then would you like to come in?"

Bloom stood her ground on the doorstep. "I'm afraid I'd rather you come with me."

Ruby cocked her head to the side. "And you're *certain* I'm not under arrest?"

"I am. Is that not enough? I'm not sure who you'd like me to check with. I give you my word that I have no intention of arresting you at this moment. That could change based on new information, of course."

Ruby waved that off and reached for her thick black

sweater on the hook by the door. "As long as you give me that nice cell with the softest cot..."

"I've already told you that isn't a cell, that's my office."

"Ah, well, as long as you arrest me and throw me in your office, I'll take my chances. Come Clifford." The hound rose from his place by the hearth and loped out. Ruby shut the door behind her, locked it with one of the few spells she knew, and followed the sheriff down the porch steps.

"I hope you haven't been telling people that when I was forced to arrest you for trespassing, I let you stay in my office," said Bloom as she nodded and waved congenially to a family of leprechauns headed the other way on the small cobblestone lane. The smallest of the bunch, toddling slowly beside his mother, looked more like a gnome than anything, with a little round nose and squishy cheeks flushed from the cold.

The mother leprechaun returned the sheriff's smile, but as soon as her eyes jumped to the Fifth Wind, she hurried her wobbly toddler along.

"You know I don't talk to anyone," Ruby said, sparing the passing family little thought. "And if I did, I definitely wouldn't tell them that Clifford and I got the VIP treatment in jail."

"Either way," said Bloom, "I regret releasing you on good behavior."

"Mmm... Yeah, I don't know why you did that. I believe, when it comes to trespassing, I'm what's considered a repeat offender. I don't know what you expect of me. Thorough investigations go hand in hand with minor broken laws. You know that."

"I have no idea what you're talking about." The angel raised her nose in the air. "Angels are... well, angels. If there was one thing Heaven valued most, it was following the rules."

"Explains why you left."

Bloom shot Ruby a sideways glance, then chuckled. "Maybe I ought to deputize you. Make it official."

Ruby gasped, scandalized. "You would never! Me, a deputy? Why, I'd never get another client again. You'd send me straight into poverty if you did that! No, I much prefer the occasional arrest followed by a sleepover in your office."

Bloom nodded. "That *was* pretty good cocoa we had, wasn't it?"

Ruby agreed and then took in the changing surroundings. They seemed to be making a beeline not for the part of town where the Sheriff's Department was located, as Ruby had expected without realizing it until then, but toward Fluke Mountain and Widow Lake.

As a mental exercise, she tried to puzzle it out before asking the obvious question. Fluke Mountain was where Zax and the rest of the werebear sleuth lived, and she wasn't especially keen on heading there at the moment. However, she and Gabby *had* worked together to solve a case on the mountain not long ago, after a few of the werebears claimed they'd been attacked by a resurrected legendary ancient minotaur. The notion had seemed far-fetched, even for Eastwind.

Maybe there was a new development with it. Perhaps another attack.

Unlikely, though.

She considered the question further: on their way to

Fluke Mountain, they would pass by multiple entrances to the Tearnanock Estates neighborhood, an invisible community of elves where she and Gabby had teamed up to stop a deranged killer.

While the land up in Tearnanock had proven to be beautiful enough, she'd hoped never to return to that place. Those who lived up there, away from what they considered the riffraff of town, were annoyingly elitist and themselves not any better than any other Eastwinder.

When she, Bloom, and Clifford passed the last invisible entrance to the elven neighborhood (that Ruby knew about, at least), she was glad to rule it out as a possible destination.

Widow Lake presented an interesting prospect if that was where they were heading. One particular geographical feature of the lake was a long peninsula jutting out into the middle of it, narrow for most of the way, then expanding in a wide circle at the end. (It reminded Ruby of a dangling uvula.) And on that wide circle of land in the middle of the lake sat an old castle, one which housed Eastwind's only vampire…

"Are we paying Count Malavic a visit?" Ruby asked, voicing her final guess to this mini mystery.

Sheriff Bloom scoffed. "Thankfully, no."

"Damnation! I really thought I had it. Where are we going, then?"

"To the other side of the lake."

Ruby considered it. "What's on the other side— Oh. *Oh!* No Gabby, we're not really going *there,* are we?"

The sheriff nodded pensively. "Afraid so. I just received an urgent owl from Beatrice Ryker, the head healer. There's been a murder at Veris Bluffs Asylum."

Chapter Four

"And you're sure it's a murder?" Ruby asked as they drew closer to the lake. The cobblestone street leading from town had just ended, continuing on by a well-worn footpath of packed pebbles.

"Can't be sure yet, I haven't seen it. But I'd say that a vampire lying dead with a stake through her heart is probably murder."

Ruby's mouth fell open and she exchanged a quick look of shock with her familiar. (At least, she was pretty sure it was shock on Clifford's face. His eyes and jowls were so droopy, it was difficult to tell.) "A *vampire*? Did you just say there's a murdered *vampire* in Veris Bluffs?"

"Technically," said Bloom, "it's a *vampiress*, but I believe most are okay with using the masculine form of the word for all genders."

Ruby continued to gape at the angel. "I'm not so much hung up on the gender of the noun as the noun itself. Gabby, why on Mother Earth do you need me to come along if it's a vampire? They don't have spirits. I can't imagine what use I'll be."

Bloom shrugged. "I might not have the power of Insight like you do, but I've seen enough things in my immortal life to know that something is off with this one. And when something is off, what do you do?"

Ruby nodded, understanding. "You get someone who is also *off* to help you out. When was the last time a vampire besides our beloved and most noble Sebastian Malavic was in Eastwind?"

The sheriff's expression tightened. "That's the thing. Never, as far as I know, and I know quite a lot. Malavic entered the realm early on, and he's made it his business to keep this a one-vampire town."

"Made it his business?" asked Ruby. "Sounds like messy business."

"I'm sure it has been. But my job is to protect the people of Eastwind, not necessarily those who come in from elsewhere seeking trouble. And besides, Deputy Titterfield and I have enough on our hands without fending off vampires. We're happy to outsource where we can."

Ruby motioned to herself. "Clearly."

Widow Lake appeared clear and blue just ahead, but before they reached the edge of the peninsula, Bloom said, "This way," and pointed to a small footpath veering off in the opposite direction of Fluke Mountain. Ruby had never noticed it before, but why would she? She'd never had the desire to visit Veris Bluffs Asylum, the place where Eastwind's chronically unwell went to heal their ailing and restless minds or to be simply stowed away from the rest of society when those ailing minds led to violence.

Bloom lead the way as the path entered a thick bit of forest. Clifford took up the rear, keeping his nose low and active with only occasional breaks to look up and verify some small bit of information he'd gleaned from the ground.

"I assume you're been to Veris Bluffs before," Ruby said.

"Many times, unfortunately."

"Not a pleasant place, I assume."

"Half of it is," the angel explained. "Not everyone who goes there stays for life. Sometimes even the sweetest, most sane folks you know come upon troubles and need a little escape and an extra bit of help. Between you and me, about half of the time anyone around town says they've just returned from a holiday in Avalon, they've actually just returned from Veris Bluffs."

"I didn't know it was so common."

"No one outside of the staff and me does. Which is probably why everyone keeps lying. It's not my place to reveal the truth for anyone else, but I often wish people would open up about it. There's nothing to be ashamed of, really. Life is hard. We need other people. And sometimes we need other people more than other times. When Eastwinders feel afraid or unable to reach out for the help they need from friends and family, there's always the rolling acres of Veris Bluffs to turn to."

"I wish someone had told me about this much sooner," Ruby said, taking care to step all the way over a fallen log to avoid ending up facedown in the cold dirt.

"You remember the state I was in after things fell apart with Ezra Ares?"

"How could I forget?"

"I could hardly talk to any neighbors about the specifics of *that* situation."

Gabby Bloom arched a brow. "Because of Ezra's illegal dealings?"

"*Allegedly* illegal dealings," Ruby corrected, though her tone had no teeth. "We don't know for sure."

Bloom rolled her eyes.

"My point," the witch continued, "is that I could have used someplace like what you're describing with Veris Bluffs. Would have been preferable to the *other* ways I went about coping with that breakup." Ruby shook her head. "And to think, I'd always considered the asylum some sort of impenetrable fortress for the criminally insane."

"Ah," Bloom replied, "but remember how I said *half* of it is pleasant? The other half is exactly what you describe. And, unfortunately, that's the half I most often frequent in my line of work. A lot of evil magic behind those walls. I won't even get started on the things I've seen in the dark entity ward. Terrifying... and a bit confusing."

When they emerged from the cover of the forest, Ruby found herself stepping out onto the edge of an expansive, well-manicured lawn. Despite the chill in the air, it had turned into a bright, sunny day with a clear blue sky, and Ruby took in her very first look at Veris Bluffs Asylum.

"I'll be hornswoggled," she said.

Clifford padded up beside her. *"Like night and day."*

"Good and evil, more like."

And indeed, that just about summed up the split nature of the scene ahead of them. The structure was massive, but split down the middle in construction, with one side made of a bleak gray stone—windowless, ancient —while the other side more closely resembled an expensive Parisian estate with red brick and white limestone, large windows and wrap-around verandas. An old, stubborn gray stone wall surrounded the dreary half, no doubt spelled to high Heaven with protective charms —not to keep anyone out, but to keep everyone in. But the luxurious half had no wall, not even a fence. Instead, across the green lawn it had a scattering of smaller buildings—this one a stable, that one perhaps a studio. And out on the grass near the pleasant part of the asylum was a smattering of Eastwinders engaged in a variety of activities—painting, meditating, even simply lying out in the sun.

"Is that Thaddeus Whirligig riding a unicorn?" Ruby exclaimed.

Bloom chuckled. "It sure looks to be."

Ruby shook her head. "Siren's song! Why am I here with you to investigate a murder when I could be riding a unicorn instead?"

Bloom shrugged. "A series of poor life choices? And besides," she addressed Clifford then, "can you imagine her atop a unicorn?"

Clifford shook his big, shaggy head, and the sheriff grinned.

"It must cost a fortune to stay here," Ruby said.

"Not at all. It's free."

Ruby whipped her head around. "Free? You just

mean the prison part, right? Well, of course *that's* free to stay in."

"No, the whole place is free to any who need it."

"But how?"

"A private donor," said Bloom. "Anonymous. It's been this way from the start, so I assume by now that donor is long gone and there's some sort of endowment set up."

"Hmph. I've definitely been missing out, then. Maybe after we discover why there's a dead vampire in this place, I ought to take a little trip here myself."

"It's not a vacation spot, Ruby. It's for mental health."

"Vacations *are* for mental health. By the way, in what half of the asylum did the murder take place?"

"That's a good question. Head Healer Ryker didn't specify."

It was a bit of a walk down a stony path cutting through the lawn before they reached the front of the structure. The path split, one side leading to a fortified iron door on what Ruby now thought of as The Bad Side of the building, and another leading to a wooden door with inset glass on The Good Side.

Bloom, of course, never one to take the easy route, lead the way up to The Bad Side.

Some people were just like that, Ruby mused, following a few steps behind the angel. They were themselves good, and because of that, there was something deep within them that was attracted to darkness, like the north and south poles of a magnet. Bloom came from Heaven with a gravitational pull toward Hell.

Ruby wondered where she herself fell within this

dynamic. She wasn't good, precisely, though she did hope to do the right thing when she could. Why? She couldn't say, especially when the wrong thing often felt exponentially better to do.

But the wrong thing always had its own natural consequences, didn't it?

Was it as simple as that? She wasn't a good person like Bloom, but she simply didn't wish to experience the consequences of doing bad things?

Perhaps not everyone was built to be a north or south magnetic pole, like Gabby Bloom and the people the sheriff pursued. Perhaps some people, like Ruby, and even Ezra Ares, existed in the middle, toward the center of the scales, sometimes a little good, sometimes a little bad, but averaging out favorably. And was Sebastian Malavic like that as well? She'd long assumed he was more like the polar opposite to Gabby Bloom, but what if he wasn't?

Why am I even thinking about that accursed man?

She put Malavic from her mind and went to stand next to the sheriff, who'd just knocked on the asylum's formidable front door. It was time to enter The Bad Side.

Chapter Five

There was a shuttering and clattering of metal bolts, and the thick door on The Bad Side of Veris Bluffs Asylum swung open. Standing at the threshold was a hard-faced woman with skin the color of roasted almonds and shiny onyx hair in a braided bun on the top of her head. Ruby suspected this woman was a witch, but she couldn't tell what kind. It was a toss-up in her mind—healing was generally the work of the nurturing West Winds, but a place like this, with such high stakes and little room for sympathy guiding decisions above practical sense, a North Wind might be better suited. The woman addressed the sheriff. "Thank you for coming."

"Of course, Head Healer Ryker. Your letter sounded urgent."

The healer's eyes fell upon Ruby and then the massive red hound beside her. "They're with you?"

"Yes, this is Fifth Wind witch Ruby True and her familiar, the hellhound Clifford True."

A sudden glimpse of uncertainty filled the healer's

hard expression. "I thought I included the species of the victim in the letter. I don't know what a Fifth Wind will be able to assist with."

"Ruby True has other talents outside of merely speaking to ghosts. I consult with her on many of my strangest calls."

That seemed to please Head Healer Ryker, who nodded succinctly. "At least you agree it's strange."

"An unknown vampire found dead in Eastwind? About as strange as it comes."

Ryker led them down a dim, unfriendly corridor with bolted metal doors on either side, and Clifford said, *"I can't imagine being in this place would make anyone less criminally insane."*

"I don't believe," replied Ruby silently, *"that the idea behind the design is rehabilitation so much as management."*

"I think you're right."

"We've certainly encountered enough beings beyond redemption, haven't we?"

"A few true psychopaths, yes. Not much you can do about those, I'll grant you, Ruby, but if even one person who's here doesn't belong, I'd call that a travesty."

Ruby patted him gently on the head. Clifford could always be counted on for wise compassion.

Ryker took a sharp right, and they entered a hallway that was cut short by two more intimidating doors. She led them through, and Ruby realized that they'd just passed the dividing line from The Bad Side into The Good Side.

Good riddance, she thought.

And yet, a part of her felt like she was somehow

abandoning those she'd just left behind in that fallow and unforgiving place. Not everyone was sentenced to Veris Bluffs for life, as Bloom had said. Some of those sitting behind the thick, silencing doors would eventually make their way out. And then what? Would they be *more* fit for society or *less*? And no system was perfect; what if some of those who had been committed to The Bad Side actually belonged on The Good Side?

There wasn't much she could do about it at the moment, she decided, and there were more pressing matters: namely, the scene they'd just come upon in the sunlit corridor.

And now it struck her just how strange it was that the murder had taken place on *this* side of the asylum. With its beautiful windows overlooking the lawn and lake, the warmth of sunbeams streaming in, and the light and airy sheer drapes hanging to either side of the windows, this was no place for murder.

Yet anywhere could be a place for murder. In fact, murderers often chose the most peaceful places to commit their acts. For one, it caught the victim off their guard. But also, it stole the tranquility of the space away from future visitors. A person might arrive, start to feel at peace, and then remember, *A murder happened here. It could happen anywhere. I'm never truly safe.*

Yes, murder was an evil thing that sent shockwaves of victimization out in all directions.

And those were the thoughts that occupied Ruby's mind when the wall of healers parted to let their boss, an angel, a witch, and a hellhound through to the dead body.

"It was good of you not to disturb the scene," Sheriff Bloom said.

The vampire was facedown on the tiled floor, her long chestnut hair fanned out in all directions. And through her back, Ruby could just make out the tip of a short, wooden stake. It was a murder, all right. The only thing missing from it, so far as Ruby could see, was blood on the checkered tile of the floor.

Ryker dismissed the other healers with a nod of her head, and Bloom was given a bit more space for her preliminary examination of the scene. She stooped down and gently rotated the victim's head around to see the face. "I don't recognize her either."

Ruby crouched on the floor next to the angel, tilting her head to look at the vampire's face straight on. "You know more than one vampire?"

"No, but there's always the possibility of a new one being created from someone in town."

Ruby gasped. "You thought it might be someone we knew whom Malavic had turned?"

"It was one possible explanation I was considering, yes."

Clifford, who had been sniffing intently around the body said, *"Look at this. Right here."*

The familiar pointed to the victim's legs below the knees, and as Ruby moved around, she wasn't sure what she was looking at. At first, she mistook the wounds for red knee-high socks.

"I thought I smelled something burning," Clifford said as Ruby got a closer look at the scorched skin.

"Holy hellhound," she breathed. "This is interesting."

"What?" The sheriff slid over to see, and Ruby motioned at the severe burns on the victim's legs. "That certainly *is* interesting." Bloom raised one of the legs to peek at the front. "The burns are mostly on the back. They reach around a bit, but they don't quite wrap around to the shins."

"Fresh?" Ruby asked.

Instead of replying, Bloom motioned for Ryker to move closer, and asked her for her professional opinion.

"Not sure how I didn't notice that before," said the head healer.

"I'm sure the discovery of a dead body held most of your attention," Bloom reassured her. "Most people don't notice all the details at once. You're unlikely to consider injuries on the legs when there's a stake through the chest."

Ryker nodded appreciatively and then allowed herself a closer assessment of the burns. "They're quite fresh. No scabbing at all. I'd say she sustained them no more than a few hours before we discovered her here."

Bloom stood. "Hmm..."

"Hmm, indeed," said Ruby, standing. She was by no means an old witch, only forty-seven as of the previous week, and getting to her feet wasn't *hard* now so much as that she was starting to *notice* it a lot more than she had in her thirties or even her early forties. She felt a sudden envy for Bloom, who appeared to be around the same age, but would never experience the persistent effects of aging. "You think it's related to the murder?"

The sheriff shrugged. "Perhaps no more than everything this woman did in her life was related, indirectly, to bringing her here, where the murder happened. I definitely have questions, though." She nodded at Ruby. "Would you like a quiet place to tune in?"

"That chair over there should be just fine, so long as I'm not interrupted."

It was time for a little Insight.

While Ruby True lacked many of the flashier skills of witches—conjuring objects and making things zoom around the room with a swish of a wand—she had her fair share of unique gifts. The gifts were ones all Fifth Wind witches had, if the books at the library were correct. But because she was the only Fifth Wind in the entire realm, she was the sole possessor of things like Insight and Quenching and Banishing. In her darker moments, when the loneliness set in, it left her feeling misunderstood and desperate, but she had to admit, having no competition *was* good for business.

Clifford followed her over to the chair in the small alcove of the hallway. It was at an angle so one could have one's back against the wall while gazing out the window, and it was a pleasant little spot. The chair itself wasn't terribly comfortable, carved ornately from a dark hardwood, but the crushed velvet cushion would provide enough support for her to focus without her backside falling entirely asleep.

The hellhound settled in as well, positioning himself protectively between his witch and the rest of the hallway. Ruby closed her eyes and relaxed her mind, trying to summon up that inner knowledge she possessed. Sometimes her deep meditations would produce from the blackness a single object spinning in space, sometimes a phrase, and sometimes an entire scene playing out. Of course, she then had to figure out what it all meant, and therein lay the problem. Was the object that had appeared to her a murder weapon? A keepsake? A physical manifestation of an emotion felt by one of the parties involved?

Her Insight only offered clues and hints, not pre-packaged answers tied up with a bow.

And so she let her mind relax, opening to whatever might be delivered to her as she focused her energy on the murder at hand. What, if anything, would reveal itself to her?

Into the dark abyss she went, feeling herself fall inward with each breath, deeper, deeper...

Something glowed in the distance and she summoned it closer.

Suddenly it was there. No, not *it*. She. She was there, standing alone in the dark abyss of Ruby's mind, transparent like a spirit but fainter. So faint. Ruby recognized the face, because she'd seen it for the first time only moments before. It was the vampire.

"Open your eyes, Fifth Wind," spoke the floating shade.

"Why should I?" Ruby asked.

"Because you don't need them to be shut anymore."

That voice had existed outside of her, she was sure, and she snapped her eyes open without another thought. There, hovering in the air ahead of her, was the very same woman.

"It can't be," Ruby breathed. "Vampires don't have souls."

"Normally," said the spirit, "I would agree with you. And yet, here I am."

Clifford was on his feet, his hackles raised as he trained a sharp eye on the new arrival.

"What's your name?" asked Ruby, squinting to make

out the wispy figure. With the sunlight streaming in, it would be tricky to see any spirit just then, but with one already so dim, Ruby might have thought she was imagining this entirely, were it not for Clifford's reaction.

"Anastasia Vorporal."

"I'm Ruby True, and this is Clifford. Do you know who murdered you, Anastasia?"

"I do not."

"But the stake went in through your front. Did you not see who held it?"

"If I did, I simply can't remember."

While it wasn't uncommon for spirits to forget details from the last moments of their life, there *was* something about Anastasia's tone that made Ruby feel like the dead vampire was holding back. But if the spirit didn't want to help Ruby out at this present juncture, there was little she could do to make her. "And where did you come from?"

"A land far away." The spirit crossed her arms stubbornly over her chest. "It's none of your business, really."

"Oh, for fang's sake," Ruby muttered. "I'm trying to help you here, dear. Why did you come to Veris Bluffs?"

"I had something to deliver to one of the patients."

Sheriff Bloom's voice interrupted the conversation. "Ruby, who are you speaking with?"

"The deceased."

Had Ruby ever seen the sheriff look so shocked? It was a gratifying moment, but she wouldn't let that distract her from the task at hand. "What were you here to deliver?"

"The object in my front pocket."

Ruby turned to Bloom. "Would you please check the deceased's front pocket?"

A moment later, Bloom pulled something truly remarkable from underneath the dead vampire and held it up for inspection. In her hand, she held a purple heart-shaped gemstone the size of a grapefruit. It glistened gloriously in the sunlit corridor.

And Ruby didn't need her Insight to tell her that the jewel was at the heart of this strange investigation...

Chapter Six

Sheriff Bloom didn't need Ruby's Insight to know immediately that this jewel was at the heart of this murder investigation, either. She wasn't sure what sort of gemstone it was precisely, but a quick trip by Ezra's Magical Outfitters would be enough to clear that up. Ezra Ares knew more about precious objects than anyone she knew. She refrained from asking the South Wind where he learned so much, since she was almost certain it would be incriminating. Most everything in Ezra Ares's immediate sphere was slightly incriminating. Nothing too alarming, and usually nothing dangerous to the public, but slightly illegal, nonetheless.

She pocketed the jewel for safekeeping and approached Ruby, as the psychic continued to converse with empty air.

Ruby nodded at said empty air, then turned to Bloom. "She says she came to deliver the gemstone to its rightful owner."

"And that is?"

"Sophia Gerards."

From behind Bloom, Ryker spoke. "Did you just say Sophia Gerards?"

The sheriff turned toward the head healer. "Yes, she did. She's a patient of yours, I presume?"

"Oh yes. Long term."

"May we speak with her?"

Ryker hesitated at first. "Okay, sure. But I don't know what exactly you'll get from her. She hasn't spoken in years."

"Doesn't mean she never will again," said Bloom optimistically. "Would you be so kind as to lead the way?"

Bloom was curious whether Head Healer Ryker would lead them back toward the high-security side of the asylum or farther into the pleasant part, and she got her answer right away: they were going to the high-security side.

A little part of her leaped with excitement, but she wouldn't let it show. It certainly made this whole thing much more intriguing. The victim was found on this side of the asylum, but the spirit claimed to have been looking for someone on the other side. It didn't add up. But neither did the lack of blood around the body. Bloom had enough experience to know what that likely meant.

As the healer led the way, Ruby caught up to the angel. "She's disappeared."

"Probably for the best. She shouldn't be here to begin with."

"It's strange, isn't it?" Ruby muttered. "Could Count Malavic have been wrong about vampires having no souls? I assume that's who you heard it from."

"He could be wrong, but then all the literature would be wrong, too. I don't take Sebastian's word on much. Not without verifying it against reliable sources."

"For what it's worth," Ruby replied, "Anastasia was faint. I've never met a more transparent ghost."

"Literally or figuratively?"

"Oh, only literally. Figuratively, she wasn't transparent at all. Her defenses were up right away. She's definitely not telling me the full truth."

"Good to know."

Once they were through the dividing doors and back into the sterile high-security hall, Ryker took a quick right and then another, and Bloom found herself in an environment she hadn't expected. For one, unlike every other cell they'd passed, the doorway at the end of the hall had a window. It was clearly a cell, but inside it was much more like the other side of the asylum, with a few high windows letting in natural light and fine furnishings throughout, from what Bloom could see from this angle.

"This is the cell of Sophia Gerards," Ryker explained.

"Hardly what I would consider a cell," Ruby replied. "More like a luxury suite."

"Yes, well, Sophia is a unique case. She's Veris Bluff's only waif."

Ruby's eyebrows shot up toward her thick orange curls. "Waif? And what is a waif?"

Bloom wasn't sure either, but she wasn't about to let her ignorance show. No point when Ruby had done the work for her.

Ryker lowered her voice in a way that made it clear this was a sensitive topic. "She's half-dead."

"Like a vampire?" Ruby asked.

"No. Not undead. Half-dead."

Bloom followed up with, "A half-dead what, precisely?"

"Skarbnik."

Ruby chuckled. "Now I think you're just making things up."

Ryker's expression hardened. "I'm not. Skarbniks are very well known in other realms."

"She's not from here?" Bloom asked.

"She's as from here as anyone is. She's a long-timer. She was here before I started working as a healer's assistant."

"Skarbniks are immortals, then?" Ruby asked.

"No. But waifs can't die. At least, I've never heard of one doing so. They suffer from a soul leak. Over time, their soul slips away, until they're left without one."

"Again," Ruby said, "like a vampire?"

"No. She's not *undead*. Just *half*-dead."

"And soulless?"

"Who's to say?" Ryker replied. "I have no way of knowing how much of her soul has leaked from her by this point."

"And why is she on this side of the asylum?" Bloom asked. "Is she dangerous?"

Ryker folded her arms across her chest and cast a quick glance in the direction of the cell door. "No, not as far as we've ever seen. The security, as I understand it, is to keep her safe more than to keep others safe from her."

Bloom perked up. "And what do you need to keep her safe *from*?"

But now the healer shrugged. "Not sure. It's been

part of the instructions for her since long before I got here."

"And that cell," Bloom continued, "it's not a usual one, is it?"

"Not at all. The only one of its kind here."

"Specially made?"

"I've always assumed so."

Ruby True tapped the toe of her soft-soled boot lightly on the flagstone floor. "Strange that an asylum for the criminally insane would have a luxury suite, don't you think?"

"I do," replied the healer bluntly. "I've always thought that."

"But you've never questioned it?" Bloom asked.

"Oh, sure I have, here and there, in the spare seconds between urgent matters that require my attention. There's not a lot of time to *wonder* when you're in charge of a place like this."

"Ah, yes," Sheriff Bloom said, forcing a smile. Ryker's growing agitation would do them no favors. It was clear the woman didn't like not knowing so much about a part of her dominion, and the questions exposing that ignorance were jabbing straight into that particular sensitivity. But they needed Ryker's assistance if they stood any chance of investigating properly. "I understand. I know many of the people on this side of the building, considering I was the one who put them here. You certainly *do* have a lot to manage."

That seemed to lessen the head healer's defenses. And Bloom wasn't just blowing smoke up Ryker's cauldron, either. She imagined the woman was telling it straight when she said she didn't have time to wonder about something odd that was not an immediate danger to anyone. In a lot of ways, Bloom lived the same reality. Except, *catching* criminals, rather than merely *containing* them, *did* require plenty of wondering.

"Could we speak to Sophia Gerards?" Ruby asked, and then before the healer could repeat herself, added, "I understand she might not say anything, but I'd still like to meet her."

When they entered, Bloom didn't see anyone at first. And then she spotted the waif huddled in a large bed in the corner of the room, hardly more than a tiny lump under the thick downy quilt that hung low over the edge of the bed, dragging on the ornate woven rug covering that entire quadrant of the cell. The whole set-up looked more like the guest bedroom of one of the expensive mansions in Hightower Gardens than anything else.

"Sophia, dear, you have some visitors," Ryker announced.

The figure on the bed didn't move.

Is she dead? wondered Bloom.

The sheriff crept closer, fearing they might now have a double homicide on their hands.

But then there was a slight stirring, and slowly the waif turned toward them.

Her eyes locked onto something then shot open wide, and Bloom turned to look behind her. The waif, if seemed, had homed in immediately on Clifford.

Bloom looked back at Sophia. It wasn't fear in the girl's eyes—and though she was likely in that twilight cusp between girl and woman when she'd become a waif, in her weakened state she much more resembled a child. Sophia stared at Clifford with unmistakable excitement.

"Ah," said Ryker, "it seems she's interested in your dog."

"Not a dog," Ruby corrected on impulse. Then, "Is it all right if he lets her pet him?"

"Fine by me."

Clifford trotted up gladly to the bedside and rested his shaggy head on the edge of the mattress. Sophia pushed herself to sitting and rested a hand gently on the top of his head. Only then did Bloom see just how pathetic a sight the waif was. Whatever a Skarbnik was, she looked almost indistinguishable from your average witch insofar as height and limbs. But this girl was practically skin and bones, and her eyes, though locked onto the hellhound at her bedside, had a clear vacancy to them. Her hair hung in dark strands down below her shoulders, and though she wasn't quite as pale as a vampire, she wasn't far off.

"She does love hellhounds," Ryker explained, sounding more maternal than she had thus far. "She even keeps a stuffed one around for— oh. Oh dear." The healer hurried over to a chair in the corner that was occupied by a large stuffed animal. The red fur and large paws made the creature it was intended to be unmistakable, especially when a much larger version of it was in the room for a direct comparison. But when the healer held up the toy hellhound, Bloom saw immediately what the cause for concern was. The stomach of the stuffed beast was torn apart, the fluff pushing its way out through the tear.

"Sophia," Ryker said, "what happened here?"

But the waif only kept petting Clifford's head, staring

at him like it was love at first sight. (He didn't seem to mind.)

"Does she destroy stuffed animals often?" Sheriff Bloom asked.

"Not at all. She's had this one for years. I can't remember a time when she didn't have it, actually."

"Another thing about her that predates you," Ruby said idly.

Ryker examined the toy from all angles. "Oh, I think we can stitch it up. Yes, this isn't unfixable by any means." She addressed the mute girl again. "Don't worry, dear, I'll get him good as new and back to you before you know it."

Cautiously, Ruby approached Sophia. "You like him? His name's Clifford. He's my familiar. He does love a good scratch behind the ears." And then, to Bloom's surprise, Sophia switched from petting Clifford's head to scratching him behind the ears. The waif was listening after all.

Ruby put her back to the patient. "Upon communicating with the spirit of the deceased," she began as Ryker's eyes widened at the new information, "I learned she was within your walls to deliver something to this particular patient of yours. Any idea how the deceased might have gotten inside?"

Ryker shook her head. "None."

"Are records kept of who comes into and goes from the asylum?"

"Yes. Strict ones. They appear in our ledger the moment someone sets foot through the door."

"Either door?" Ruby asked.

"Either. Either of the front doors, the back door, and the emergency exits as well."

Bloom asked, "And the windows?"

"No ledger for that," said Ryker, "but it does set off an alarm loud enough to wake the dead."

Sheriff Bloom nodded. "Very well, then. That leaves us with yet another mystery. How did she get inside without appearing on the ledger or setting off the alarm? This might take a bit more asking around than I'd hoped, but I'm sure we'll figure it out."

Ryker nodded. "However I can help, Sheriff. It wouldn't do for word to get out that someone had found a way in, and thereby a way *out* of Veris Bluffs undetected."

"No," Bloom agreed. "The last thing anyone needs is a rumor circulating of a possible break out from here."

Sophia Gerards continued to pet Clifford with that blank expression, only now there seemed to be the hint of pleasure tilting up the corners of her lips. This *was* a strange scenario.

As Bloom turned back toward the door, she spied Clifford give the waif one final sloppy lick on the wrist. Then the group, save the patient, said their goodbyes and stepped back out of the lonely room.

"I'll need to speak with your staff," Bloom said. "All of them."

"Of course," said the head healer. "If any of them had anything to do with—" But she didn't finish her sentence. Her face went blank like she'd just seen a ghost.

The sheriff had an idea of what it was she *had* seen, but it wasn't a ghost.

"Ah, Ted," Bloom said, confirming her suspicion as soon as she turned.

He stood where the hallway forked, one way leading him to where they now stood, the other leading toward the doors into the nicer half of the facility. "Heh, I guess I came in the wrong side."

Gabby Bloom grinned at the grim reaper in his dark hood, his scythe gripped in his hands about as non-threateningly as one could hold such a weapon. "You did, I'm afraid, but we're just about to head back to the body, so you're welcome to join us and we'll show you the way."

"That'd be great. Heh."

As he joined the rest of the group, giving Clifford a welcome pat on the head as soon as the hellhound was within reach, Bloom said, "I will ask you to hold off on gathering the spirit for the journey on, Ted. Just the body will do for now."

"The spirit?" the reaper said. "I didn't sense any spirit."

Bloom and Ruby shared a glance, and the sheriff let the Fifth Wind take the lead in explaining. "That's because it's a strange sort of spirit."

"All spirits are a little quirky," he said. "It's one of the things I love about this job! Heh."

"Just wait," Ruby said. "You'll understand better once you see the scene."

When they arrived at it a moment later, Ted stood beside Anastasia, looking around. "Where's the body?"

"It's, um, it's at your feet, Ted," Bloom said as kindly as she could.

"I know *this* body is here. But she's a *vampire*. You

said something about not collecting a *spirit*. Whose spirit?"

"It's *her* spirit," Ruby explained. "There was only one murder that we know of, and it's this vampire. I spoke with her ghost myself."

Ted used the pointy tip of his scythe to scratch his skull through his hood, creating a noise that made nails on a chalkboard sound like sweet lyre music. "That just can't be. Vampires don't have spirits. They have no soul. They just die and that's that. It's why I've never had to guide any to the next life. They don't go anywhere."

"It's a unique situation," Ruby conceded. "But it's the situation nonetheless."

A whimpering sound like a rusty door hinge came from beneath the reaper's hood. "Oh *no*... Does that mean I'll have to reap Sebastian Malavic when he dies? I was *so* looking forward to having a friend I didn't eventually have to reap."

"Don't worry," Sheriff Bloom assured him, "I'm fairly certain that man is entirely without a soul. As Ruby said, this is a unique situation and goes against most of what we know about vampires. But it's all part of the fun mystery."

"Heh. I guess so," Ted said, sounding slightly cheered.

"Now, if you don't mind attending to the body," Bloom continued, "I have a few people to interview, whose souls I'll inspect for guilt. Ruby, you and Clifford are free to return to town. Meet at A New Leaf in three hours for a debrief?"

Ruby grinned. "Making me return to my favorite tearoom, eh? Twist my arm, why don't you. Fine, if you insist, Clifford and I will head there *right away*. Just in case you finish up here early."

The Fifth Wind and her hellhound made toward the front door of the pleasant half of the asylum, and Bloom hollered after them, "For Heaven's sake, don't eat all the chocolate croissants before I can get there!"

And Ruby tossed over her shoulder, "I'll do my best, but I'm not an angel, remember."

Chapter Seven

Just over three hours later, Sheriff Bloom stepped into the tearoom and let her eyes adjust to the light. An unexpected storm had blown in an hour after Ruby had arrived at A New Leaf—likely a result of some North Wind witch training at Mancer Academy—and the sheriff paused to stomp the sludge from her boots before proceeding across the warm, dry space.

The sheriff had hardly pulled the chair out to sit in it before Harley Hardtimes was there, setting a warm chocolate croissant on the table in front of the angel.

Ruby grinned mischievously then winked a thank-you at the older witch. Perfect timing.

Bloom's eyes grew wide and greedy before a grin blossomed on her lips. "You saved me one."

Harley Hardtimes chuckled. "Not just one. I'm baking a fresh batch right now. Almost ready. Thought you might like some treats to take back to the office with you."

Ruby suspected the sheriff's professional demeanor

was only hanging on by a thread when she replied, "Yes, Mr. Hardtimes, I believe that sounds like an excellent idea. To share, of course. Deputy Titterfield loves these as well." And then as soon as the owner had nodded and stepped away, she added, "He doesn't. I'm going to eat them all myself."

"I know," Ruby replied. "One of the many benefits to not gaining a pound no matter how much you eat."

Bloom waved her off. "That's just a fallacy. I can gain weight. Plenty of portly angels in Heaven. I just get too much exercise to ever pack on the pounds. Flying expends much more energy than you'd think. And in a storm?" She shook her wings, sending excess droplets onto the carpet beneath the chair.

"Shall I let you get that first bite in before I start grilling you?"

"Oh! Yes, please do."

Bloom enjoyed the first taste of the warmed croissant so much, Ruby hardly had the heart to interrupt her at all. She considered letting the woman finish it in its entirety and move on to a second but found she couldn't wait.

In the hours since Ruby had left the asylum, a hundred new questions about the situation had started to form in her mind, swirling around like a tornado of impatient uncertainty. "And? Any guilty suspects?"

Sheriff Bloom wiped a smudge of warm chocolate from her cheek and sucked it off her finger. "No, nothing at all. Ryker couldn't have hired a more guiltless group if she'd tried. A bunch of saints, those healers."

"You don't sound thrilled with that," Ruby said

amusedly. "I assume it's not because you don't want those in the care of Veris Bluffs to receive the finest treatment."

"Of course it's not that."

"So, what now? We have a dead vampire from who-knows-where with a spirit—who-knows-how— carrying a gem that means who-knows-what."

"Don't forget the waif who's been in the asylum since who-knows-when," Bloom added. "I think the first place to start is this." She pulled the purple gemstone from her pocket and held it up. "It's strange, isn't it?"

"In many ways. The least of which is the natural heart shape."

The precious stone took up most of Sheriff Bloom's palm as she held it out. "You haven't heard from Anastasia in the last few hours, have you?"

"Not since the asylum. I suspect she doesn't want to be questioned."

"Suspicious." Bloom pocketed the gem again for safekeeping.

"Just like everything else about this case."

"Who do you think might know more about this gem?" asked the sheriff.

"Your guess is as good as mine."

"Sometimes, yes," Bloom said. "And sometimes it's worse."

"And sometimes it's better," Ruby added, taking a quick sip from her hot tea. "The trick always seems to be figuring out whose guess is better when."

Bloom popped the last of her pastry into her mouth and pulled the gem back out, staring down at it as she chewed. Then she said, "I believe I might have a good guess coming together."

"Then yours is probably better than mine. What is the guess?"

Rather than answering, the angel asked another question. "What price you suppose a gem like this might fetch?"

Ruby arched her eyebrows, catching on. "You think Ezra is the person to speak with?"

"If anyone has seen one of these before, it would be him, don't you think?"

Ruby nodded. "You think it's powerful."

"It certainly feels that way. Or at least like it used to be. There's an echo of magic to it, but it feels... I don't know how to describe it. Here. You take it."

Ruby did, and the instant the stone's weight entered her palm, she understood. "It's like it's dead. But it's a rock, so clearly it was never *alive* in the strictest sense of the word. Yes, I see what you mean. I believe Ezra might be able to help us."

But that, of course, meant that she would have to see Ezra today.

Her gaze dropped down to her open palm where the heart-shaped stone still lay, powerful once, now dead. Cold. Snuffed out.

Ruby finished the last bit of her tea then called to Clifford to join her. She turned to the Sheriff. "Business is business, I suppose. Speaking of which, we never discussed payment."

Bloom got to her feet quickly. "Right, right. How about we discuss that on the way?"

"While my lips are frozen shut? Pah! I'm onto you, Gabby."

The angel laughed. "You are. That keen mind is why I bring you on."

"And why you'll pay me twice the usual fee this time around."

Bloom shot the Fifth Wind a sideways glance as the women (and Clifford) made their way toward the door. "I thought a visit to Ezra's Magical Outfitters would sweeten the deal enough for you."

"Oh, hush you. In fact, maybe we shouldn't speak at all on the walk over there."

Chapter Eight

In contrast to the crispness outside on that November day, the air inside Ezra's Magical Outfitters felt stifling and hot.

And those were two words Ruby never thought she'd associate with the place: stifling and hot. The shop usually felt bright and airy with its tall, glass exterior, open rows of display cases, and massive amounts of ambient spellwork, the kind that put shoppers in the mood to spend far beyond their budget.

Clifford had opted to stay outside, not because he didn't want to see Ezra, but because he *always* found the place a bit stifling with its magic. After all, the high-end shop was filled with nothing but magical objects. If a witch desired her first wand or needed a new one, there was no better place to come than here. Looking for a new broom? Ezra had that covered as well. Need some protective amulets to fend off dark entities? Well, who *didn't* now and again? Ezra had the fix for all of it.

For a long time, this had been Ruby's favorite shop,

and not just because of who she got to see each time she entered. But now?

Sheriff Bloom took extra care stomping sludge off her boots on the front mat while Ruby quickly located the person they needed to speak to across the showroom floor.

Ezra Ares was in his element. Ruby recognized it well. He had a mother and her teenage son totally engrossed in his pitch as he held up one of his finely crafted wands, twirling it slowly to allow the light to glisten off the wood glaze.

Where was he in the sale? Was he still explaining all the dangers one might face by scrimping on a lesser wand, or was he already explaining all the benefits of shelling out just a few extra coins to make sure the young witch would finish top of his class at Mancer Academy?

Bloom stepped forward and Ruby put out a hand to stop her. Judging by the witch mother's face, Ezra was about to close the sale. It would be a real crime to intervene when someone was using their talent to such an enchanting effect.

Ruby had every intention of waiting patiently to the side until the money had been exchanged, but a quick sideways glance from Ezra derailed that plan. His eyes lit up when he spotted the new arrivals, and he interrupted his own pitch. "Ruby True and our very own Sheriff Bloom!" He waved them over to where he stood with the mother and son. So, he wanted her help, did he?

This was an enjoyable pastime she and Ezra had done a thousand times together as well…

Ezra said, "Mrs. Rainy, Timothy, this is my dear friend Ruby True. And you know the sheriff, I'm sure."

Mrs. Rainy appeared slightly stunned to find herself in the sudden presence of the Fifth Wind and the angel, but she nodded anyway. "Yes. Sheriff Bloom and I spoke at the Lunasa Festival a few months ago."

Gabby Bloom wagged a finger. "That's right! You were giving me your creamed corn recipe, weren't you?"

Being remembered seemed to please Mrs. Rainy, and she grinned and nodded.

Ruby weighed her options. On the one hand, she was here on official business, and teaming up with Ezra would be a distraction, not to mention unfair to Mrs. Rainy and her son. But on the other hand, helping Ezra close the sale would be a good bit of fun...

She opted for fun. "Wow, that's quite a wand you have there, Timothy."

"Oh," Ezra said, slipping into their familiar rhythm without a moment's hesitation, "it's not his, I was just showing it to him."

Ruby gasped. "But I could have sworn... The magic flowing between the wand and the witch is remarkable!" She shook her head. "I don't mean to sway you, Timothy. This is a big decision. This tool will obviously make or break your magical potential for years to come. I've seen witches rush into it and pick the wrong wand then spend the next twenty years essentially waving around your average twig and hoping it'll do their bidding!" She addressed Ezra, "The Quixote girl did that, you remember?"

Ezra nodded solemnly. "Oh yes. I remember."

"Quixote?" asked Mrs. Rainy. "I'm not familiar with that name."

"Ah," Ruby said, "that's because she was the last of

her line. May she rest in peace. Really could have used the right wand when facing down that vicious hellhound." She snuck a quick glance at Ezra, who was expertly biting back a smile.

Timothy's eyes, meanwhile, had glued themselves to the large, dozing hellhound just outside the front of the store.

It wasn't always a hellhound that the Quixote girl was eaten by in this routine. Sometimes it was a dragon, sometimes a hidebehind, and sometimes a spell merely backfired on her. Ruby had always liked to switch it up, keep it fresh.

"Don't worry," she added once it was clear both mother and son had let their imagination run wild enough, "she only ended up with that useless twig because she refused the one Ezra had picked out for her in favor of a *cheaper* one. Were the coppers saved worth it to her in those final moments? Who can say? But I *will* say," Ruby continued, "that I haven't seen a connection as strong between a wand and a witch, like the one I'm seeing right now, outside of the High Priest Clearbrook himself!"

"You can *see* the connection?" the boy asked timidly. "I didn't know witches could do that."

"Most witches can't. But I can. It's a Fifth Wind ability. The connection happens on a psychic level." Ruby tapped her noggin as evidence and hoped neither Timothy nor his mother noticed the sheriff rolling her eyes.

Ezra held out the wand. "Here," he said, "give it a little time in your hand. See if it feels right. If I'm not mistaken, the sheriff is here on official business." He grinned up at Bloom, who had a few inches on him. "I'm not under arrest, correct?"

"Not today. Just looking for your expertise."

Mrs. Rainy proceeded to watch her son wave the wand impotently, eyeing him as if she were looking at the next High Priest in training, as Ezra led the other two across the store to speak in private.

"Apologies for interrupting you at work," Bloom began.

"Are you kidding?" asked the South Wind. "You just made me a sale I was about to lose! You should have heard how many times Mrs. Rainy asked about the price. Usually East Wind witches aren't so stingy. I might have expected that from a North Wind, but... Doesn't matter. Ruby has closed the deal for me." He winked at the Fifth Wind. "You still got it, gorgeous. Next round of wards is on me."

Despite her wishes, Ruby felt herself blush. Oh, he *was* insufferable with his charm!

Gabby Bloom grunted. "I probably should have stepped in and told them the truth."

"Fang's sake," Ruby said, waving off the angel's conscience like steam from a cauldron. "Ezra *always* picks the right wand for the witch. And it really *is* worth every coin he asks. I wasn't lying."

"There's never been anyone by the name of Quixote in this town," Bloom said.

"Okay, I *was* lying. But only about that."

She exchanged a furtive look with Ezra, who nodded approvingly then said, "What can I help you with this afternoon, Sheriff?"

Bloom looked like she wanted to say something else

about the con but skipped whatever it was. "I have a gem. I think it might have been powerful once, but I don't really know anything about it. I thought you might be able to identify it." She pulled it from her pocket and held it out.

Ezra's eyes grew large.

"What is it?" Bloom asked.

He shook his head. "I've never seen anything like this. Can I hold it?" Once it was in his hand, he turned it over a few times then held it up to the light. "You're absolutely right. It was incredibly magical. But the magic's dead in it now. It's just a rock." But he didn't hand it back. "If you need someone to take it off your hands—"

Bloom snatched it back. "I think we can handle it. I assume it's worth something still, yes?"

"Nope," he said.

"Ezra," Ruby warned.

He chuckled. "Okay, yes, I could sell something like that for a fortune. Not for the magic, though. I'd need to shine it up a bit, get that foggy exterior off it."

"Not happening," said the sheriff. "It's evidence."

"Evidence?" And now he looked genuinely interested. "Involved in a crime? I could fetch even more for it, then."

"A murder," Ruby explained. "We found it on the body of a murdered vampire in Veris Bluffs."

His eyebrows shot up.

Bloom took it from there. "The victim was apparently trying to deliver it to someone inside the asylum."

Ezra stared down at the rock in Bloom's hand. "The magic on that might be dead now, but considering we can all feel that it was there, I have no doubt it would have set off the contraband detectors if someone had brought it into Eastwind aboard the Avalonian Express."

Bloom nodded. "Good point. But aren't there *other* ways to get magical objects into this realm undetected?"

Ezra straightened up. "Sheriff, I have no idea what you're talking about."

"Oh, please. If I were going to arrest you for your regular goings on, I would have done it ages ago."

Ezra looked to Ruby for a sign. She shrugged.

"Fine," he said. "Yes, there are other ways to get things into Eastwind undetected. But I'm fairly certain I know about all of them, and if someone smuggled in something like *that*, I would have been notified immediately."

"How might someone do that?" Ruby asked.

"A portal, generally. There are a few scattered around, mostly in the Deadwoods since we've closed the others. There's one in a, um," he shot the sheriff a quick glance, "a private residence, and I don't have any ability to monitor that one. I doubt the stone would have come in through there, though. Regardless, I'm not the man you should be asking about this."

Bloom tilted her head to the side. "Who do you suggest instead?"

"Assuming that this gem has resided within Eastwind for some time, and considering the victim was a vampire... I dunno about you two ladies, but my mind goes straight to one person."

Both women groaned.

"What?" Ezra said, sounding slightly defensive. "I

thought you two in particular wouldn't mind paying him a visit."

Ruby narrowly avoided gasping as she turned wide eyes on the South Wind. That *almost* sounded like jealousy.

Only it couldn't have been, because he'd said it about Bloom, too.

"I'm not sure why you said that," Bloom replied, her words infused with an added dignity, "but you're right. A stone like this would have been easily hidden and right at home in the Eastwind Treasury."

And now Ruby did gasp. "The burns!"

"Burns?" Ezra asked.

But Bloom understood. "The dragon."

"If Anastasia went down there first to get the gem..."

"It makes sense."

Ezra's shrewd gaze jumped from woman to woman. "I'll trust you both on that."

Bloom tucked the stone into her pocket again. "Thank you for your help, Ezra. We'll leave you to close that sale."

As the women made for the exit, he called after them, "I'm serious about the wards, Ruby."

"I'm all set on them for now," she replied.

"Then how about dinner instead?"

Her heart did a somersault in her chest, and she stopped walking and turned toward him. "You know better, Ez."

He shrugged. "I had to try."

If only you'd tried fifteen years ago, she thought. But rather than saying another word, she offered him a sad smile and said, "I think your guests are ready to check out."

And then she caught up with Gabby Bloom, rejoined her familiar out in the cold, and set off to pay a visit to Count Sebastian Malavic.

Chapter Nine

109 years before the present

Though Sheriff Bloom knew whenever she was expending a lot of energy, she didn't grow tired. And that particular angelic benefit came especially in handy when she had a fleeing suspect in her sights...

The chase had begun in the Outskirts, the seedier part of Eastwind where none but the roughest of werewolves spent their time. Yet this was no werewolf leading her in this pursuit. This was a were-elk who had made the unwise decision to steal from a werewolf. A priceless decanter, if the letter arriving by emergency owl was to be believed.

When she'd responded to the scene, she'd caught this suspect sneaking into the cover of the Deadwoods, where he'd quickly shifted and fled on hoof toward the center of town.

Bloom was a swift runner, but not as swift as an elk.

Flying, though, was a completely different question.

She could fly faster than any creature could run, all while going *against* the wind.

And so she tracked from the sky, waiting until she had a clear shot to dive down and tackle the suspect. It wouldn't be a painless apprehension for anyone, but she couldn't die, and she doubted she would cause any lasting injuries to the giant elk that trained healers couldn't mend.

The suspect galloped up one of the many spokes leading to Fulcrum Park at the center of town, but the trees along the avenue provided just enough shelter to keep her from getting a clear shot. Then the elk was there, right by the fountain. Now was her time...

It was in that split second as she prepared for her dive that something hit her square in the face. It squawked, as alarmed as she was by the midair collision, and she found herself spitting out a few gray owl feathers.

Any other bird, and she would have brought about its end with a knock at that high of speed, but the owls in Eastwind had so many protective charms on them—mail tampering was among the highest of crimes—that she was shocked she managed to hit it in the first place, let alone knock off a few of its feathers. She must have been going even faster than she'd realized.

The owl flew off on its way, no doubt in a foul mood but otherwise fine, and Bloom scanned the ground beneath her to relocate her suspect.

She found him fleeing the park and making his way down a road on the other side.

She had to beat her wings hard to catch up, but she did. Just another moment, and she would have a clear shot of him... Just once he was clear of that bunch of trees...

Down she went like a lightning bolt, the air howling in her ears as she plummeted with precision.

She caught him just where she meant to, wrapping her arms around his thick middle and causing him to roll in such a way that his legs weren't in danger of any breaks as her momentum was deflected.

The suspect went down in a puff of dust from the cobblestones, and when it cleared, she located his legs and shot out her golden ropes, binding both front and back limbs together in a single bouquet of hooves.

She got to her feet to inspect the scene. One of the were-elk's antlers had broken a tine, but that would be easily mended. She might even have been able to mend it herself, except she had more important points to which to attend.

The suspect shifted from his elk form in a hurry, but she'd expected it, and with a flick of her wrist, she tightened the golden ropes to adjust to the smaller limbs as he struggled, naked as the day he was born, on the cobblestone street. A wave of her arm, and a golden cloth appeared, wrapping itself around the suspect's exposed parts, keeping him decent for whatever witnesses might show up.

"Jacob Pinehorn," the sheriff said, "you're under arrest."

The last of the dust settled, and behind the veil of it appeared a tall, pale figure, his mouth agape. Only then did she fully realize where she'd brought this pursuit to an end: right outside of Sheehan's Pub.

Sebastian Malavic snapped his mouth shut and

began to clap. "Brava, Sheriff! Damnation, what a show! Do you hold regular performances?"

Sheriff Bloom ignored him and went to grab her suspect, who rolled around and struggled against his binds between her and the vampire. "I didn't do anything!" Jacob Pinehorn shouted, his two front teeth dangling in much the same way as the tine had before his shift. "Untie me! I—"

The golden gag appeared with a lazy gesture of her hand. "Then why did you run, Mr. Pinehorn?" She wasn't mad, though. She enjoyed a good pursuit now and again.

Count Malavic drew closer. "Do you do that *often?*"

"What, catch criminals? Or cover up their personal bits with a golden cloth? Or gag them?"

"Well, I'm starting to understand that you gag them quite frequently. I meant the chase."

"It's not *infrequent*," she replied.

Malavic smirked. "And based on your heavy breathing and that smile you're trying to keep hidden, it's not *unpleasant*, either." He held up a hand. "No need to deny it, my dear sheriff. I enjoy myself a good chase as well." His tone made it clear that he was talking about something totally unrelated to enforcing the law. "If I'd known *this* was part of your job, I might have applied to be deputy just to witness it." He turned his eyes up to the blue sky. "My devil, you came out of nowhere! I have half a mind to commit a crime and flee from it just to force you to tackle *me* like that!"

"Please keep thoughts like those to yourself, Count," she said, releasing Mr. Pinehorn's legs from the ties so she could haul him up onto his feet.

"And what if I don't?" Malavic continued. "Are you going to tie me up, too?" He held out his wrists as an offering.

She paused, her eyes flickering to his hands. "Maybe. But not today." And then she threw the defeated suspect over her shoulder and took to the sky. She had an arrest to complete.

It was late by the time Gabby Bloom had gotten Jacob Pinehorn set up in the single cell of what hardly counted as a sheriff's office. The place was not much more than a broom closet with a desk connected to an even smaller broom closet of iron bars. Goddess help her if she ever needed to arrest more than three people at a time. They would end up like sardines packed in the cell until she could process them and, if she were lucky, let a few go ahead of their trial. Ironhelm Penitentiary, not normally seen in a positive light, seemed absolutely spacious after a night in the sheriff's cell.

The office, if it could even be called that, opened onto a side street a block off the Eastwind Emporium, and it was from there that someone knocked on her office door.

She looked up from her arrest logs and over to the clock. It was well past dinnertime. Normally anyone with an emergency just sent an owl. The bird would swoop in through the single high window and ring the emergency bell to get her attention. Or, if she were already out of the office, the owl would track her down. Postal owls were powerful indeed.

But there was no owl just then, only a knock.

"Come in," she said. She had no reason to fear whoever was there, though others might; a perk of being an immortal, and a powerful one with the Goddess's blessing on her side at that.

The door opened, and Count Malavic stepped across the threshold, holding something in his hand. He lifted it up, and she realized at once what it was: a bottle of wine. Dust still clung to it from where he must have procured it from his storied personal stores. "Brought us a little something to share."

"Us?" she said.

"Yes. You didn't expect me to simply drop this off without tasting this particular vintage myself, did you?"

"Why would you drop it off at all?" she said, continuing to eye the vampire suspiciously.

"I'm here to congratulate you on that daring arrest today, and it would be a strange thing for me to pop in, drop off a bottle of wine, and expect you to drink it all alone. My company is part of the gift."

"I don't suppose there are any gift return options?"

He grinned. "It's less spacious in here than I remember. Ah, well, we'll just have to cozy up."

Before she could say another word, he'd grabbed a chair, scooted it up to her desk (there wasn't far to scoot), and gently cleared off a space for the bottle and two crystal goblets he'd pulled from beneath his cloak.

She listened for sounds of stirring from Jacob Pinehorn on the other side of the cell door and was met only by a loud snore.

"Why are you really here, Malavic?"

He looked up as he pulled the cork free. "I want to spend a little time with you, Sheriff. We've known each other for so long, and yet I don't feel like we know each other at all."

"Is that the treasurer of the High Council speaking, or the vampire who lives in his spooky castle in the middle of a lake?"

"The two cannot be separated, I'm afraid." He poured her a generous portion of wine. "As much as I wish I could keep my professional and personal life completely separate like so many falsely claim they can, I'm realistic: I'm but one man, not many parts of a man. One man. And as such, the desires of that man permeate every part of my life."

He lifted his goblet, and against her better judgment, and she possessed quite a lot of it, she grabbed the goblet in front of her and raised it as well.

"To getting to know each other better," he said.

"And to such a development not forcing me to arrest you for a very long time."

He was the first to grin, but hers broke through shortly after.

Gabby Bloom brought the goblet to her lips and tasted. The dark wine was luxury in liquid form. It was buttery smooth with the hint of rich raspberry and chocolate. And at the end, just a little flick of surprise.

Bloom held out the goblet to stare at it in amazement. "Is that sparkleberry I tasted at the very end?"

"Indeed."

"I had no idea you could use sparkleberry in wine."

"It's rare anyone does. They tend to explode the cask about three months in. It takes an expert hand to manage."

This was certainly no good. Now she would *always*

want sparkleberry in her wine, and she was sure the town didn't pay her enough in a year to buy a single bottle of what she was enjoying now.

"I'm glad you like it," Malavic said, his voice as smooth as the wine. "I can tell you have a hard edge to you, Sheriff, but I happen to know that usually means there's a woman inside that could use a bit of indulgence. It's not easy to keep the emotional tides of the world at arm's length to maintain the facade of authority. I would know."

Bloom took another sip and tried not to moan. "Would you really have me believe you possess a tender inner world, Count?"

"Please, call me Sebastian. And no, I don't expect you to believe that. But it's true. I wasn't always a vampire, you know. I was a victim of one before any of my blood-thirsty tendencies arose. A normal mortal."

"Doesn't mean you weren't *also* bloodthirsty then."

"I wasn't."

"And it doesn't mean you weren't *also* a cad."

"I wasn't that either. Not by any stretch. There was only one woman for me." He waved his hand in the air. "I won't bog you down with that. It was so long ago anyhow. I hardly remember it, frankly."

But now she was intrigued. She'd never considered this aspect of Sebastian's existence. Yes, he was someone she had, on occasion, fantasized about locking away forever, but before she ever met him those centuries ago, and before he ever came to Eastwind as the sole vampire of the realm, he had to *become* a vampire. And no one she'd heard of had ever *chosen* that. It was chosen for them, *inflicted* upon them.

Could everything she disliked about him be a result of that single trauma, that original victimization? And where did it leave her? Was she supposed to feel sorry for him and forgive his current behavior in the context of his violent turning, or should she expect him to have found a way to deal appropriately with the events that had befallen him by no choice of his?

"Why tonight?" she asked. "Why drop by tonight after we've known each other this long?"

His eyebrows arched. "Shouldn't it be obvious? That display I saw you perform today. I had no idea so much went into this work."

"The sign of a successful department is that people don't notice it working, they just think the town is naturally crime-free."

"Then I suppose you weren't successful today, Sheriff, were you?"

"Gabby, please," she said. Then, when he seemed to get an idea about that intimacy, she added, "Only because I'm supposed call you Sebastian. It seems fair you should get to call me by my first name, as well."

"Everything must be fair and even for you?"

"It's ideal, yes."

"Then I'll call you Gabrielle."

"No, you won't."

He feigned shock. "But that's your first name, isn't it? You call me by my full first name, and I'll call you by yours. If I called you Gabby, I'd have to allow you to call me Bastian, which is something I don't let anyone call me anymore, not even the sheriff of the realm. Fair and even, Gabrielle."

She glared at him as best she could while the flavor

of the wine still fogged her judgment. "I'm about to rescind my invitation and have you call me Sheriff again."

"Suit yourself. I like calling you that. Reminds me of those gold bindings. Tell me, Sheriff, how bad do I have to be to get you to tie me up like that?"

She cleared her throat and sat up straight. "I have some paperwork to attend to, Count. I appreciate the wine—it's incredibly delectable—but I'm technically at work."

"When *aren't* you at work?"

"Never."

"Then that means you're also at home. I appreciate you inviting me to your home like this to split a bottle of wine."

"I didn't invite you anywhere. You just showed up."

He stood from his seat, and she thought, with some relief and some regret, that he was about to leave. But instead, he stalked around the desk and stopped just a foot shy of where she sat. Their eyes met, and she tried as best she could to gaze down deep into his conscience, to search for the guilt that may or may not stain his soul. But, of course, there was no soul to be stained, and she found herself tumbling deeper and deeper into the endless pit of his dark, sultry eyes...

His fingers, chilly to the touch, brushed beneath the corner of her bottom lip, and he stared down at his hand. So did she. There was a dark drop of the wine on his fingertip, a remnant of her last indulgent sip.

The Count brought it to his lips and licked the liquid off. He hovered over her now, trapping her with his stifling presence, and she became so absorbed in the fine features of his face this close up that she didn't have any brain left to realize how foolish she was being.

"You can tell me to leave," he whispered. "It's your home, after all."

"Jacob Pineho—"

"He's sleeping. I can hear his vile snores, and so can you." Sebastian backed off suddenly, giving her space, allowing her better nature space to flood back into her body, replacing whatever hellfire had begun to flow through her veins instead. "You've almost finished your drink. And I mine. There's plenty more in the bottle, though. Would you do me the honor of sharing another drink? Maybe we can talk about something more to both of our tastes this time?"

"I can't imagine a thing that would be to both of our tastes," she replied.

He filled up her goblet first, then his own, leaning close to her as he did. "Oh, I think there's plenty. Vengeance, for a start." He handed over her refilled goblet and leaned against her desk, still staring down at her.

Bloom hesitated, knowing what another glass, another conversation, would mean after she'd been working so hard for so long and without a lick of companionship to break up her days and nights...

She should have sent him away, but instead, she brought the goblet to her lips in that cramped office, and before she took her next sip said, "Well, I *am* an avenging angel. I love a bit of vengeance here and there..."

"Excellent," said the Count. "Vengeance it is."

Chapter Ten

❧

Presently

Ruby True had been to Count Malavic's castle a number of times before, but she was never *not* awed by the sheer size of it, especially close up, as she was now.

Sheriff Bloom, Clifford, and she had just made the long walk down the neck of the narrow peninsula stretching out into Widow Lake, at the end of which resided the castle. The group approached the front door, and Ruby reminded herself why she was here. The gem, the treasury, the burns on Anastasia's legs. Ezra was right, those pieces did connect right back to Count Malavic.

Then again, the count tended to have connections to every case she investigated, even if he wasn't directly involved. He attracted bad intentions and seemed to end up in the middle of them whether he meant to or not.

You didn't always feel that passionately opposed to him, said a goading memory in her head.

Clifford growled low. *"Please, let's not talk about that right now."*

"Stay out of my thoughts, Cliff."

"I'm trying. But those were very loud and aromatic ones."

And why were they visiting her now? Of all the times she'd visited the count at his home, only once had it gone *that* way...

It must have been the conversation in the tearoom that left her feeling somewhat soft for him. Or perhaps the visit with Ezra had turned an old stone.

Sheriff Bloom took the lead and knocked on the solid wooden door of the castle, then stepped back. Almost immediately a shower of red sparks exploded in the air in front of them, causing Ruby to jump a half-step back.

"Harp string," cursed Bloom. "Looks like Deputy Titterfield needs me right away. He almost never calls for backup."

"Oh, *that's* what the sparks were about?" Ruby said. "Very well. You handle that. I can deal with Malavic myself."

Bloom passed off the gem, and with a nod but not another word, spread her wings, leaped into the sky, and soared away.

Ruby watched her go until the sound of the door opening behind her pulled her attention away.

"Such a pleasant surprise, Ruby. And Clifford, of course. What's one without the other? What can I do for you two?"

Ruby stood up straight, trying to convey some of the authority she'd lost the moment of the sheriff's winged departure. "I need to speak with you regarding a suspicious death in Eastwind."

Malavic forced a smile. "Of course you do. What else would bring you here? Oh wait, you haven't broken up with Ezra Ares, *again,* have you?"

"Hush! Why would you even mention such a thing? That was years in the past, Malavic. Dead and buried."

"You and I both know that the dead can remain unburied for quite some time, Ruby." He stepped to the side, holding open the door. "Come on in and ask me your questions. Shall I open a bottle of wine?"

"I'll hex you if you so much as try it."

He chuckled and closed the door behind the witch and her familiar.

They settled into a glum sitting room that wasn't dusty but had the heavy feel of age settling upon it, and Malavic clasped his fingers together in his lap as he sat opposite Ruby and put on his best, most convincing listening face.

It wasn't all that convincing.

Ruby took a moment to find a comfortable position on the crushed red velvet love seat that was more like a long footstool with a rigid backrest. Once she was settled, Clifford sat smartly at her feet, putting himself between his witch and the vampire, and keeping a close eye on the latter.

"Ask away, my most welcome guest."

"For the record, I'm here to address the treasurer of the High Council, not the vampire Malavic."

"Who can say where one ends and the other begins? But if you're here for a loan, I'm happy to provide. You've always seemed like a sound investment to me, Ruby. If you only bent your rules of ethics here and there, you could make a *fine* living as Eastwind's only psychic, you know."

"I make just the living I intend to, thank you. And I'm not here for a loan." She pulled the gem from one of the deep pockets of her black robes and held it out. The moment Malavic's eyes landed upon it, his face changed. She could have sworn there was fear in those hollow eyes. Then, in a flash, the chasms closed up, and he reached forward, took the large rock from her hand, and held it up to a sliver of light cutting between the closed curtains.

"You recognize it?" she asked.

"No."

"It sure looked like you recognized it just now."

"Looks can be deceiving. You must have mistaken my surprise at seeing something *this* valuable plucked from robes such as yours for recognition. I only recognized the value of the thing."

She ignored the slight. "You know what it is?"

"Of course. I could tell right away. It's a raw periwinkle sanguinite, I'd bet my life on it."

"You mean that as a figure of speech, I'm sure. We discovered it on the body of a murdered vampire within the walls of Veris Bluffs Asylum earlier this morning." She watched him closely for any small movements that might give away his true reaction to the news (if it *was* news to him at all) but the vulnerability she had glimpsed a moment before had only fortified his defenses, it seemed, and he showed no indication of anything suspicious.

Instead, he said, "A dead vampire? Couldn't be. I'm the only one in Eastwind, and I'm feeling quite healthy today. Or rather, as healthy as a vampire forbidden from drinking the blood of his neighbors *can* feel."

"It was a vampire, I'm sure. She was there to deliver this particular gem."

"Yes, I see the logic you're following. And I'll spare you further suspense. I believe you might be onto something in coming to me. While it would be absurd to expect me to recognize every valuable rock and coin we keep within that treasury, I will say this is highly likely to have come from the stockpile. It has a few key markings, which I won't bore you with, but yes, I believe this was recently property of the township of Eastwind. Do you need to hold onto it as evidence, or shall I return it to the caverns?"

Ruby considered it. "I don't love the idea of walking around with such a valuable item in my pocket. So as long as you can put it somewhere where we might easily retrieve it later, should more inspection be required, I don't mind you keeping it. But one more question. If this was recently under the protection of your dragon and guarded below Rainbow Falls, how on earth might the dead vampire at Veris Bluffs have gotten ahold of it?"

Malavic's next words sounded particularly measured. "A very good question. One that might be worth investigation, don't you think?"

"Of course. That's why I'm—"

"Let's go now."

"Go?"

The vampire was already on his feet. "Yes. Let's pay a visit to the treasury, you and I—and Clifford, of course —and we can take a look around, see if we find any hints as to how this gem"—he held it up—"ended up on a murdered vampire."

"Ah. I see."

"Unless you have something more pressing to attend to this evening. Perhaps dinner plans with a gentleman suitor?"

She pressed her lips into a thin line. "You know I have nothing of the sort. But I *am* getting a bit hungry."

"Then we'll stop for a snack on the way. Shall we?" He held out the crook of his arm.

Ruby stood, smoothed out her robes, and glared at the count's proffered elbow. "We shall, but if you think I'm going to be seen promenading through town arm-in-arm with you, I'd say the centuries alone have officially addled your brain."

He shrugged. "Fair enough. But have you ever considered that it would be *my* reputation that took the greatest hit by being seen walking arm-in-arm with *you*? Everyone would think I'd lost my edge."

"I would never want that for you, Sebastian, so we'll make sure to keep a proper distance."

And as they left the castle, Clifford was more than happy to walk between them, enforcing a distance that Ruby herself didn't actually feel all that inclined to maintain...

Chapter Eleven

9 years before the present

Would this ache in Ruby's chest ever stop? Would the words spoken by the first man she'd loved ever cease to haunt her? It was impossible to imagine that reality now, only a day after they had been spoken.

Ruby sulked shamelessly by a roaring fire in the hearth of A New Leaf, Clifford curled up on the pillow beside her chair, his big body overflowing the cushion so that his head rested across her feet.

She could hardly taste the aromatic blend of her tea, and though she knew Harley Hardtimes made everything fresh and kept it warm, the croissant on her plate tasted stale and flavorless in her mouth.

The brutal truth had pounced upon her like a hidebehind on a lone traveler in the Deadwoods: Ezra wouldn't age. The years they'd spent together had been full of mischief, excitement, and a feeling that Ruby had never experienced before, that someone was there for her no matter what. Ezra would have her back in a fight whether she was right or wrong, and that meant something. She was more important to him than being right, let alone lawful.

But she wasn't more important to him than his own youth, it seemed. The splinter between them, subtle at first, had come into clear relief this last year as she noticed her first grays and realized he never would have grays of his own; but still, she'd hoped that he would change his mind, agree to grow old with her.

That was all anyone wanted when it came down to it, wasn't it? Someone to grow old with. But not while only one was growing old and the other was staying the same age.

Ruby knew better than to fall in love with an immortal, and Ezra wasn't one of those, even now, but she hadn't known he'd desired to be. She, so attuned to death, so at peace with the notion that it would someday be her spirit who crossed over (though she hoped she didn't need the assistance she so often rendered others), Ruby True, the lone Fifth Wind witch in the entire realm, had fallen madly in love with the one mortal most terrified of death.

And so, she'd *had* to end it. Or had he dealt it the final blow? That was the trouble with an ultimatum, wasn't it? One person eventually reached that point first and presented the option, and the other made their choice. Who was responsible for the end, then?

She reached down and stroked her familiar's soft head, staring at the hearth flames as they danced. Would it feel better to tell herself that she had been the one to end it the moment she gave the ultimatum to choose either a life with her or continued youth? It wasn't as if she'd been without a clue which one he'd pick.

But she'd still hoped he'd surprise her.

We'll never grow old together.

"I'll grow old with you, Ruby. You won't be alone forever."

The hellhound earned himself a solid scratch behind the ear for that. *"Will you be okay, Cliff?"* The hellhound had befriended Ezra's familiar, a tall gray cat with two orange tufts at the top of each ear. She didn't know hellhounds and felines could become such fast friends. The cat, Scarlett, had kept Clifford engaged with lively and iconoclastic conversation during the long days and nights Ruby had spent with the familiar's witch. In other words, Ruby wasn't the only one feeling the loss in the tearoom just then.

"Of course I'll be fine," Clifford assured her. *"And so will you. We still have each other. You know I'd fight to the very edges of the realm to stay with you."*

Ruby felt a tear spring free, and she wiped it away hurriedly and resisted the urge to bury her face in the soft fur of her familiar's neck while she was in a public place. *"I know, dear friend. I would do the same for you."*

The unoccupied chair next to hers by the fire was suddenly, noiselessly occupied, and she looked over to see who had joined her.

She almost didn't recognize him. The compassion and concern on his face made him appear like a complete stranger.

The new arrival leaned forward to place a cool hand on top of hers on the armrest of her chair. "Are you all right? I've never seen you look so down."

Surprised to find she had no gut urge to pull her hand free from the touch of Count Malavic's, Ruby replied, "I'll be fine eventually."

His face darkened. "It's that Ares fellow, isn't it? I knew Ezra was reckless, but I only thought it was with trade laws, not a fine woman's heart."

Fine woman's heart? Now she was suspicious. She pulled her hand free. "Since when have you ever considered me that?"

"Always, Ruby. I've kept a close watch on you since you first entered town. For obvious reasons, death fascinates me. I'm afraid I'm a little obsessed with it."

"That explains your friendship with Ted, but I'm afraid I'm very much alive."

"But death follows you."

"And he follows you, too. I've seen the pair of you leave Sheehan's together plenty of times."

"I'm not talking about Ted."

She sighed and turned her attention to the fire. "I know. But what I don't know is why you're here."

"Have you ever considered that perhaps I really *am* the philanthropist some in this town believe me to be?"

"What, because you throw money at things you want to control? Please, Malavic, I'm not a charity, just a fool. Fools don't deserve charity anyhow."

"Call me Sebastian, please."

"No thanks."

"Why are you suspicious of me?"

The question was enough to force Ruby to look at him. In the orange glow of the firelight, he didn't look his usual pale self, and it almost felt as if she was looking into a human face, one she might find handsome if it belonged to a different mind and heart. "Why *wouldn't* I be suspicious of you?"

"You believe my motive for coming over here to speak to you to be impure?"

"I would be shocked to my core if it were anything else."

"Then prepare to have your knitted socks blown off and your gorgeous red curls stick straight out," he said, just a hint of a smile on his lips, "because I came over here to speak with you solely because I thought you might need a friend."

She inspected him closely. "A *friend*?"

He nodded. "And as your potential friend, I wholeheartedly encourage you to stop drinking tea and switch to something stronger instead."

It wasn't the worst suggestion, she supposed. "Harley doesn't carry anything stronger."

"Then we'll have to go somewhere else instead. Sheehan's, perhaps?"

She leaned closer to him so no one might overhear. "Sebastian Malavic, are you trying to get me drunk?"

"Absolutely. But only as a friend might." Yet nothing about the grin that curled his lips spoke of mere friendship.

"A friend! Bah! I've met men like you before." She sat back in her chair.

"And did you have a night to remember with them as well?"

Her stomach hopped like a were-bunny. "I thought the invitation to alcohol was intended to help me *forget*, not *remember*."

"That depends on how wholly you commit yourself to the undertaking."

She narrowed her eyes at him. "You're not my type."

"I do expect that's the main appeal of me. I'm not your type, so there's zero risk of this leading to you falling for yet another man who won't age."

She shot him a dirty glare, and he held up his hands. "What, am I incorrect in my assessment of the situation? Did I guess wrong on why you're sitting by the fire like an old crone lamenting the better days gone by? My dear Fifth Wind, you still have *so* much living to do."

She tipped back her mug only to find she'd reached the dregs. Feeling revived, whether from the tea or the conversation, she made up her mind. "One drink at Sheehan's Pub. But you're paying—"

"Of course."

"And you will *not* accompany me home after. No gentlemanly overtures. I'll see right through them, you understand?"

The count grinned victoriously. "I understand. I will not accompany you back to your house afterward."

"Are you sure this is a good idea?" Clifford asked. *"Alcohol is not known to make anything better the next day."*

"It's just one drink. I've made my boundaries clear. And it might be nice to think about something else for a few hours."

So Malavic paid for her tea and croissant and followed her out of the tearoom.

The entire month of January had been a bitter one, and today was no different. The icy wind felt like a series of paper cuts across her face, and she pulled the hood of her wool jacket up over her head, tightening the draw string at the bottom.

The count paused once they were outside and the winter chill blew between the tall shops, waiting for Ruby to properly adjust her outerwear. Then he offered her an elbow. "Considering the weather, I believe I might be a warm improvement."

And because she thought it might be nice to feel a firm, protective body up against hers, even one that lacked as much heat as the vampire's, she accepted the offer of his arm, clasping her hands around it and letting him tuck it, and her, close to his side as they made their way through the cruel wind on their way to the pub.

It was such a relief to step inside the dark, stagnant interior of Sheehan's, out of the relentlessly whipping winds, that she almost cried and shouted with joy. She refrained, though, and settled on a soft smile instead.

"Feeling better already," Malavic said, slipping his arm free of her grasp, and placing a firm hand on the small of her back. "Glad to see my plan is beginning to pay off." With gentle pressure, he guided her toward the bar ahead of him.

Clifford had opted to remain outside, not at all bothered by the weather, since none of it could penetrate his thick coat, and the hellhound, like all hellhounds, ran a little hot anyway. Every familiar Ruby knew about opted out of entering the pub and being forced to either stand the whole time or lie down on the perpetually grimy and sticky floors. And perhaps for that reason—the absence of familiars—Sheehan's Pub was notoriously a place of bad decisions.

Malavic motioned to the leprechaun behind the bar

who nodded and scurried off to a back room while Ruby found two empty stools at the bar top. While she usually went for a quiet booth, she thought remaining out in the open was her best bet for a visit with Malavic. And besides, those moments in the quiet booths, set away from the rest of the drunkenness, hidden in shadows, were ones she'd spent with Ezra Ares, and the whole point of coming here was to forget that.

Chaney the leprechaun returned a moment later carrying two wine glasses and a bottle of red without a cork, which he set on the bar in front of Malavic.

The vampire grabbed the bottle and held it up for Ruby to view the label. "This wine comes from the—"

She held up a hand to stop him. "Please, spare me the history lesson. I'm going to drink the stuff, and I'm sure it'll be delicious. Just pour it."

To her surprise, he refrained from presenting her with a comeback and did as she asked without further comment.

The wine was beyond delicious; it was heavenly. The very first sip washed away all hope she had of only having one glass of it. She might never taste its equal again. It was like drinking buttery grapes, if such a thing was possible. She looked down at the glass as the final flavor kicked in. "Is that... sparkleberry?"

The count nodded. "It is."

"I've never had a wine with sparkleberry in it before."

"That's because—"

"Shh..." She pressed a finger to his lips. "I don't care why. Like I said, I don't need a lecture on the wine."

Their eyes met, and she removed her finger quickly,

worrying she'd just crossed a line that wouldn't be redrawn until the morning.

"I know we're here to help you forget about that idiot South Wind who didn't know what a good thing he had going," Malavic began, "but I'm dying to know: What did you ever see in him?"

"He's exciting," she said without hesitation. "He made me feel alive. When he wanted to do something, he just did it. And when the thing he wanted to do was technically illegal, he merely saw that as an obstacle to work around."

"You liked that he was a criminal?"

"I liked that he was determined. Is determined. For fang's sake, Sebastian, he's not dead! Let's not speak of him in the past tense."

"He's the past tense for you, though. And good riddance. He's a fool. To pick youth over something true, if you'll forgive the pun. Only a fool would do that. I would have killed to grow old with the woman I loved."

Ruby gasped playfully. "You loved someone? No! Not the dreaded Count Malavic!"

"It's true. But that was a very long time ago. Things change. I've changed. And then again, in a lot of ways, I haven't changed much." He sipped his wine with a devilish grin.

"Do you think you'll love again?" she asked.

He didn't need to think about it. "No. I don't think I will."

"That's a lonely prospect," Ruby reflected.

He tilted his head and narrowed his eyes at her. "I just said I'll never *love* again. I didn't say I'll never share my bed with someone again."

Ruby's face felt suddenly flushed, and she suspected it wasn't merely from the wine. "That's certainly an interesting approach."

He leaned forward, clasping his glass between both hands. "A fascinating one, if I do say so. And an effective one."

Ruby cleared her throat and considered leaving, but there was still wine left. "I can't imagine you don't feel lonely *sometimes*."

"I do, but doesn't everyone? I mean, look at you. You fell in love and it didn't save you from loneliness, did it?"

When she couldn't find a retort for that, he quickly added, "But maybe you don't feel lonely right now. You have a friend with you to share a drink. Let's change the subject to something happier, shall we? Tell me all about the latest dead person in Eastwind."

The dark humor was enough to lighten the mood, and Ruby was surprised to find herself falling quickly into easy conversation with the count, of all people.

While she regaled him with a tale of her most recent client, he nodded along, delighted, and refilled her cup almost without her noticing. The wine was like dessert, and she indulged. But unlike most reds she'd tried, it didn't weigh her down, but lifted her spirits, buoyed her such that none of the events of the last twenty-four hours stood a chance of pulling her back under into the mood she'd entertained at the tearoom.

She hardly noticed when the second bottle arrived.

Chapter Twelve

Presently

"And would you know if another vampire entered the realm?" Ruby asked. Just off to the right of where she, Clifford, and Malavic walked was a large, emerald pasture where half a dozen unicorns grazed quietly beneath the setting sun.

As promised, they'd stopped by a shop in town to grab Ruby (and Clifford) a bite to eat before heading to the treasury. Ruby finished the last of her raisin cookie and dusted off her hands before sticking them into the warmth of her coat pockets.

"How do you mean?" Malavic asked. "Some special vampire power where I would sense another one of my kind within proximity?"

"Yes, I suppose that's what I mean." And feeling a bit foolish, she added, "This is all part of being a thorough investigator."

"It's not as dumb of a question as you may think. Vampires can sense *some* other vampires when they're within the same realm. It's a developed skill though, and it only applies to one's own sire or the vampires one goes on to sire, their progeny."

"And if that were the case, you would feel, what, a little tingle in your fangs?"

He arched an eyebrow and shot her a sideways glance as they proceeded down the road. "Something like that. I likely wouldn't know if, say, my sire appeared in Eastwind. But I would feel it if said sire appeared in Eastwind and was, for instance, particularly angry. Those strong emotions, the kind that make my sire's blood pump faster through her veins, those are the ones I would feel coursing through my own blood."

"*Her* veins?"

"Yes."

"Your sire was a woman?"

"Unfortunately, yes. But it was so long ago as to be irrelevant now. Some young vampires stay with their sires for centuries, learning from them, benefitting from the protection of a stronger and more capable being. I fled from mine. But again, that was centuries ago and a world away."

"So, then the name Anastasia Vorporal means nothing to you?"

He considered it silently. "No, doesn't ring a bell."

"Hmm..."

Ruby was prepared to walk the rest of the way to Rainbow Falls, and the treasury beneath it, in silence, gathering up her thoughts and the various threads, none of which seemed to tie together at this point, but the Count had other plans. "Have you spoken with Zax Banderfield since this morning?"

"Zax?" Ruby hadn't thought of the werebear in hours. "No. Why would I have spoken to him?"

"Because if he had half a brain, he would have spoken to *you*. He would have sought *you* out and told you it was nothing serious with the elf Filaemenia and that you were the only woman he had any interest in spending time with."

"Only if that were how he actually felt, which it clearly isn't." She hoped to change the subject, but she did appreciate Malavic's flattery.

"The fact that he hasn't done it yet isn't proof that he doesn't feel that way. It's only evidence that he's a dense idiot lacking in manhood."

"You sound surprised."

"Hardly. I've served on the High Council with him for years now. He bends to public opinion like a sapling in the wind."

A sound like a flute filled the air briefly, and the unicorns stopped their grazing and began trotting back in the direction of the sound, getting ready to turn in for the night.

"Isn't the High Council *supposed* to do the public's bidding?" Ruby asked.

"If we did, there wouldn't *be* a High Council any longer. We're to do what's best for the public, not to do what they believe is best. Those are vastly different ways of thinking."

"You know what's best for Eastwinders then?"

Malavic shrugged shamelessly. "I know what's best for their money, yes. It's among the reasons I have so much of it myself."

"Financial sense, is that what you claim to have? I thought you were just a miser."

"That, too. And yet, I'm also the town's biggest benefactor, so save your judgment, witch. I can't tell you how long it's been since I didn't have to supplement the town's income with some of my own just to get a few things done around here."

Ruby rolled her eyes. "Please, Sebastian, don't play the martyr with me. We both know you don't give without occasionally asking for things in return. The town owes you a huge debt, literally, and that means you get to do as you please."

He grinned. "It does, doesn't it? Small price to pay."

Clifford scented the air, and a few paces on, Ruby caught the smell of running water as well. The sound of the falls had crept in slowly without her noticing, and now that she tuned into it, she could hear its loud crashing on the rocks at the bottom. A few more paces, and she caught sight of the edge of the bank, where the water sparkled in the dusk rays, casting glorious rainbows in the mist where it tumbled over the edge of the cliff and became Rainbow Falls.

"We're going in through the front," he added, and soon Ruby was inching down a worrisome rocky path. She kept one hand on Clifford, whose four legs afforded him stability she lacked, and was starting to fall into a rhythm when the large stone under her right foot rolled out from under her. She stumbled to catch herself, but the rock where her other foot planted went the way of the first, tumbling down the slope.

She was falling, was going to tumble right into Malavic and take him down with her into the freezing water below.

But in a heartbeat, and before she could utter any note of a cry, the vampire turned and was there, arms wrapped around her, holding her steady.

Ruby swallowed hard, still envisioning the dreadful next few seconds she'd narrowly escaped.

"Careful," came the count's rich voice in her ear. "Who's going to solve this case if you end up at the bottom of Widow Lake?"

She leaned her head back to stare into his face, and a delicious memory from years before flooded her brain. She could almost taste the sparkleberry flavor of that wine...

Mustering strength from unknown places, she pushed herself free of the count's arms. "I appreciate your sudden concern for law and order. I'll be more careful the rest of the way down." Immediately, though, she felt the loss of his body against hers.

It was curious how a body like his, usually cool by comparison could feel suddenly warm and inviting when the weather was especially frigid. Comforts were always relative, she supposed.

Her legs ached from the atypical use as she finally made it to the bottom of the steep incline. They were now on a small, rocky footpath around the edge of the lake, and the full force of the waterfall stood ahead of them.

Freezing droplets swirled in the air around her, sticking to her skin and threatening hypothermia if she didn't get somewhere dry soon. "We don't have to go *under* that, do we?" she shouted, struggling to be heard above the roar of the falls.

"Fangs and claws, no," Malavic replied. He pressed his hand to a nearby boulder, and a doorway appeared in the side of the cliff. Ruby gaped at it, and once she and Clifford had followed the count inside, she said, "I suppose I know one way the thief could've gotten inside the treasury, now."

"Fortunately, it only opens to my hand. And I would never let in someone I didn't trust. And a vampire at that! Not a chance. I know vampires too well." The door disappeared behind them, leaving them in total darkness.

Had there been even an ounce of remaining light, Ruby might have been able to Quench it, to bring it from the outside in so that she could navigate the hallway without running straight into something solid, but the place was pitch black. They were shut in underground.

"Take my hand," said Malavic. "I can see just fine. I expect Clifford will be able to follow us without much trouble, but you might as well get a handhold on some of his fur, just in case."

"I'm fine," Clifford insisted. *"This place is like a tomb. All kinds of preserved smells. I'll be able to find my way after you."*

"If you insist."

And so the vampire led the Fifth Wind hand in hand through the dark tunnel, stepping carefully, adding an occasional direction of, "There's a large rock coming up, stay right behind me so you can keep that shin of yours unbroken," and the like.

Suddenly, he pulled up short, and Ruby nearly ran straight into the back of him. "What? What is it?" she whispered.

"It just occurred to me..." Sebastian Malavic spoke in deep, rich tones that seemed to surround her entirely in the closed space. "If you sent your hound away, you and I could have quite a good time in here, and no one would ever have to know. It's dark enough that you could imagine me to be whomever you chose."

Clifford growled.

"Fair enough," Malavic said. "Just a thought."

"A thought that would have been better kept to yourself," Ruby added as firmly as she could, even while something bounced and bounded in her chest.

Zax had *never* tried anything so brazen with her. Were it anyone but the count...

Or maybe he has a point. No one would need to know...

Clifford's wet nose jabbed her firmly in the small of her back, and she took the hint and forced the fantasy from her mind.

Though it *was* nice to be wanted by someone, especially when a part of her was beginning to wonder if she was about to age out of the dating pool all together.

Malavic led her on.

A glimmer broke through the darkness up ahead and creeping beams of light danced on the tunnel's walls. Finally, they stepped out of the darkness and into a massive cavern filled with piles and piles of valuable and invaluable objects. Hovering orbs cast warm illumination over the space, bathing not just coins and gems, but what appeared to be a variety of powerful artifacts, each of which rested on its own marble pedestal. Some were under glass, others behind a shimmering magical barrier, and still others appearing to have no covering at all, which probably meant a nasty spell had been put in place instead to repel any potential thieves.

And then she remembered: there was a dragon guarding this place. But where? She looked around but didn't see anything resembling scales among the glimmering bounty.

"Stay close to me, and you'll be fine. I know this place well, and Maggie would never harm me or my guests."

"Maggie?" Ruby asked. "Your dragon's name is Maggie?"

"Why not?"

She didn't have a good answer to that.

Clifford padded quietly behind her as the count led the way through the main chamber and into an adjoining one equally full of riches. *"Explain to me again,"* Clifford said, *"how Eastwind doesn't have enough money to clean that ancient clog out of Fulcrum Fountain?"*

"I wish I could, but I can't. I had no idea we were sitting on this much wealth. These caverns must reach for miles."

"They would give those of the library a run for the title of most cavernous underground structure."

To Malavic, Ruby asked, "Are all of the contents the property of Eastwind?"

"No, no. Most of this is privately owned wealth."

"Privately owned by whom, specifically?"

He cast a grin at her over his shoulder. "Me."

She shared a wide-eyed look with her familiar.

"The place where I believe this gem of yours might have originated was just around this bend here."

The ground beneath her feet shook, and she stopped in her tracks and looked around.

"It's just Maggie," Malavic assured her. And a moment later, a large, scaled head appeared around a bend, smoke issuing from the nostrils. "Darling," he declared, opening his arms to the great beast who stomped over. The dragon was easily forty feet from the tip of her tail to the smokestack she called a nose, and despite the count's cavalier attitude, Ruby found herself looking around for a place to hide should the dragon need to, say, sneeze.

Hot and cold met as Sebastian Malavic wrapped the dragon's head in his arms and rubbed a hand over her scales. "Some women like that I'm cool to the touch," he said, stepping aside and motioning for Ruby and Clifford to come forward. The hellhound was just fine staying put, but Ruby thought it best to play friendly with the sentient flamethrower, and she approached as cautiously as she could without showing fear.

"Maggie," he began, "this is Ruby True and her familiar Clifford. They're friends of mine and are allowed to be here, so please no roasting, understood?"

To Ruby's amazement, the dragon nodded.

"Can I pet her?" Ruby asked. "Would she like that?"

The count didn't have to answer, because the dragon nodded again, and before Ruby could even believe it, she had her hand on the smooth scales of a dragon in the middle of a treasure hoard. This job *did* take her to some strange places!

Malavic produced the gem again and held it up to Maggie. "Do you recognize this?"

The dragon tilted her head like a confused puppy.

"Ah, that's all right. I can't expect you to remember every object in here."

But it was too late. Maggie backed up, her head low, tucked her leathery wings close to her, and sulked off.

"I said it's all right! You don't need to—" Malavic sighed. "Ah, well, I'll give her a treat later today and she'll realize I mean it."

Ruby was almost afraid to ask. "A treat? What does that look like for a dragon?"

"A live unicorn, of course."

Ruby gasped.

Chuckling, Malavic added, "Only a joke. She's a vegetarian. She enjoys a specific variety of birch that Thaddeus Whirligig grows. It's got just the right crunch that she loves. I'll have someone levitate one down for her. Just over here, now."

Finally, they arrived at a pile of gems that *did* have the same coloration as the one found on Anastasia's slain body, though none carried the same heart shape as far as Ruby could see. But rather than adding it to the pile, Malavic waved his hand and a stone pedestal rose from amid the front of the pile. He placed the heart-shaped stone atop it with a reverent delicateness then stepped back, keeping his eyes glued to it.

Ruby stepped forward to stand shoulder to shoulder with him. "Why the pedestal? Is it somehow special?"

He turned to her. "You don't know?" His eyes carried a heat in them that surely must have been her imagination...

It nearly stole her breath. "Why would I?" she managed to ask.

"That gem has fate written all over it." He closed the space between them, and a craving to meet him in the middle stirred inside her. What *was* this wildness, this poor judgment that had taken root at the tearoom that morning, that had reached back in time to fasten itself to that single night of abandon the two of them had shared? And why couldn't she shake it?

"Fate?" she managed to whisper.

"Don't you feel it? Fate that I was there when that oaf and his sorry companion entered the tearoom this morning. Fate that you were called away to a murder that required you to return to me. Fate that your only lead brought us to be alone in a cavern when the one thing that can distract you from your pain now is the same thing you turned to the last time."

"We're not alone," she said, trying to fight it. "Clifford's here."

"And I know exactly how to drive him away." Finally, he pulled her into his arms. "You know it doesn't have to mean anything with me. Just a delicious distraction for both of us. You from your heartbreak, me from this unending loneliness. Just say yes."

She tried to turn her head to check on her familiar, but the count pressed a hand to her cheek, turning her attention back to his blazing eyes. Only an instant, though, then she felt his lips upon hers, and the coldness of them sent a chill down her spine.

Ruby pulled herself free for air after an eternity and was all but ready to accept the vampire's delicious invitation, when a figure appeared behind him.

The spirit of Anastasia hovered in the empty space of the cavern, easier to see now in this dim light but still hardly more than a wisp. "It's him," the ghost said, her eyes wide in horror. "I remember now. He's the one who murdered me."

Chapter Thirteen

Ruby stared at the count, trying to reconcile the spirit's warning with the man who'd just kissed her so passionately.

It wasn't *that* hard to do.

She knew who she was dealing with here, a vampire who would have no problem taking a life if the occasion called for it. He could be both that and the man who had won the heart of a dragon and had wrapped her up before she could fall down the side of the cliff. Sebastian Malavic could be many things, and he'd proven time and again that he was all that and more.

"Don't let on," Clifford advised from where he stood behind them in the dim caverns of the treasury. *"Don't let him know what you've heard."*

Though only a moment before, she'd wished for a little privacy from her familiar, now she was thoroughly grateful for his stalwart presence of mind.

The ghost of Anastasia Vorporal spoke again. "I can't

stay much longer, but you need to get away from him. He'll kill you."

How do you know? Ruby wanted to ask.

"What?" said Malavic. "What is it?"

He had seen the confusion in her eyes, the doubt. Ruby might not have said anything stupid, but she was sure her stunned expression had spoken volumes.

"You were about to say yes," Malavic continued, "to indulge us both. I know it. But now... something changed." He pulled his head back further while keeping his arms around her. "Damnation, it's not that oaf werebear, is it?"

"No," Ruby managed to say, "it's not Zax. It's not anyone. I promised to meet Sheriff Bloom shortly to tell her anything I might have discovered about the gem."

"So it *is* someone else. But not the one I thought." He tilted his head to the side, his predator's pupils still large with lust. "You're afraid she might find out what we're about to do and think less of you." He chuckled. "I can assure you, in this matter, the angel has no room to judge."

"It's not that, Sebastian." Ruby mustered the control to push free of his arms. "I have a job to do. A woman was murdered, and I need to find out why. This diversion won't do." She patted her hair back into place. "I'd appreciate it if you'd lead Clifford and I out of here."

The count was quiet for a moment, inspecting her much more intently than she liked. "Very well. The offer stands, however. You know where to find me when this investigation concludes. Or, if you get the itch for an expensive bottle of wine sooner, you're welcome to come by... assuming I haven't found someone else to preoccupy myself with."

"You really are a cad," Ruby said, trying to sound exactly as she might had she not just learned he was *also* a murderer. "Now, if you would, please lead the way out, Malavic."

And so he did.

By the time she and Clifford made it to the sheriff's office an hour later, Ruby's adrenaline rush had crashed and she was hurting for a little tea. But it would have to wait. Because her investigation had taken a sharp turn the sheriff needed to know about.

Bloom wasn't at the station when she arrived, but Deputy Titterfield was and offered to send an owl for the sheriff to return as soon as possible. His offer of coffee while Ruby waited was tempting, but it was late, and the last thing she wanted was to spend the entire night awake, thinking in circles about this strange day.

Titterfield picked up on her state, though, and made an offer of the other beverage they kept in store: chamomile tea.

That was much more her speed, and it was as her hot mug had finally cooled enough to drink that Gabby Bloom arrived through the front doors of the station, looking as composed and in control as usual.

She held up a finger to Ruby as she passed her in the waiting room and continued to Deputy Titterfield's office, where she leaned her head in. "Darby Habershire claims he saw a hidebehind lurking near his property. Little odds of one being outside the Deadwoods, let alone allowing itself be seen by someone as unobservant as

Darby, but I told him you'd follow up with him tomorrow to make sure it doesn't come back."

With that settled, she nodded for Ruby and Clifford to follow her into her office. She closed the door behind them and took a seat behind her paper-strewn desk. "I understand you—"

"Sebastian Malavic murdered Anastasia."

"Oh, for Heaven's sake." Bloom groaned. "That's what I was afraid of."

"Really? You thought he might have done it?"

"Of course. How do you think he's kept this a one-vampire realm? It's not by tracking them down and asking them nicely to leave." She paused. "How do you know it was him?"

"Anastasia appeared to me in the treasury right as... right as we were returning the gem to where it belongs. She said plainly that she'd remembered who'd murdered her, and it was him. Count Malavic."

Bloom crossed her legs and leaned back in her chair. "Did she use his name?"

"I don't believe so. It was, um, so surprising to see her there, I can't remember exactly." Ruby avoided meeting Bloom's eyes.

"Yes," the angel said, "I suppose that likely was a bit of a shock." She slapped her thighs and stood. "It doesn't look like there's any way around it. I have to go arrest Count Malavic for murder. This is going to go over *great* with the charities and institutions he supports."

Ruby blinked. This was happening very quickly. From kissing the count in the cave to letting the sheriff arrest him on murder charges in under an hour.

It could never be said that Ruby didn't flirt with danger, but still.

"Wait." Ruby hurried to her feet. "What if it was, I don't know, justified?"

Bloom paused at her office door and turned back to face the Fifth Wind. She arched a single eyebrow like a bowstring. "It almost sounds like you don't *want* me to arrest him. Is there anything else I should know, Ruby?"

"Nope. Nothing."

Bloom caught her eye for only an instant before Ruby diverted her gaze. No good letting the angel get a sharp read on her guilt today.

"Do you smell something?" Bloom asked suddenly.

"Smell? No. What does it smell like?"

A small grin tilted the corners of the sheriff's lips. "Strangely like a bunch of unicorn swirls." She chuckled. "Please, Ruby. I know the signs. You can't hide *that* from me."

"It was only a kiss! He made the first move. I ended it."

Bloom held up her hands. "Listen, for once, no judgment from me. But I still have to arrest his hide for murder."

"Of course."

Bloom looked ready to leave but paused again. "If you want to sneak into his cell for a little—"

"Oh, *stop* it, Gabby. Fly on out of here and arrest him already."

Chapter Fourteen

109 years before the present

Gabby Bloom hated coming here. The High Council's chamber was an obnoxiously grandiose rotunda stretching out fifty feet in all directions with a clock tower at the center. The curved edges were smooth stone walls, and on one side rose seven marble daises, each a dozen feet tall with marble stairs spiraling down around it. Upon each one sat one of the seven members of the Council.

Bloom had no choice but to come today. She had to face the facts: after twenty-six days straight without even an hour for her restful meditation to help organize her mind, it was clear she couldn't keep doing this job on her own.

The seven members of the Council looked down at her from their high seats as she concluded her verbal appeal. It wasn't the first time she'd come begging, and she was sure it wouldn't be the last.

High Priestess Stratus was the first to speak. "Your request makes perfect sense…"

The muscles in Bloom's shoulders began to let go.

But then the priestess finished with, "…from your perspective. However, I'm here to represent the Coven, and as such, I need to consider their perspective above all else. I haven't heard a single one of my witches complaining about crime lately. That tells me that you've found a way to keep it all under control. I'm not sure what we would be funding, then, if we did give you the money you requested. Less non-existent crime? Stopping crime before it happened? That's hardly very judicial. Even I, in all my power and glory, cannot predict exactly what crime will happen, when, and where with any certainty that I would place the power of the law upon."

"I understand, High Priestess, and I would never come here to ask for help arresting Eastwinders before they committed any crime. That doesn't seem right to me either. All I'm—"

"If you could argue ill health effects of your current routine, I would support your request, Sheriff." It wasn't the High Priestess who spoke this time, but Kenneth Cormac, a leprechaun. Bloom opened her mouth to remind him what she had said in her initial appeal about not having had a moment to meditate in almost a month, but he cut her off. "However, I understand angels are immortal. You cannot, then, claim that the stress of the job is hurting your over-all life expectancy, and that's the root of all health concerns, isn't it? That ill health will kill you before your time. But you *cannot* die. See my logic, Sheriff?"

Bloom silently prayed to the Goddess for the strength

to keep from rolling her eyes, and it only just worked. "It might not kill me, Councilmember Cormac, but over time, I believe it has diminished my capacity to do my job to the best of my abilities."

And now it was Abernathy Stormstruck, the head of the werebear sleuth in town, who spoke up. "I do believe the High Priestess has already established that your performance is stellar. Like her, I haven't heard any complaints about crime from my bears. Therefore, I simply can't justify the expense of adding another officer to the payroll."

Gabby Bloom trained her eyes on one of the Council's immortal members then, hoping *he*, at least, would understand that just because a situation couldn't kill one didn't mean it couldn't be a royal pain in one's hide.

Liberty Freeman, the only genie in the realm, and a man she quite liked on a personal level, had listened to the arguments with a quiet but unmistakable engagement, and now he sat with his thick arms folded across his chest. He was not her best hope for an ally here, considering he tended to believe much more should be legal than was, but that was hardly her fault. She was the law *enforcement* not the law *maker*. If he took issue with what was and was not allowed, he had no farther to look for the responsible party than himself and the other six council members gathered around him.

Somewhat predictably, Liberty said, "It sounds like you're responding to every small spat, no matter how minute. Surely there are calls you respond to that could just as easily be handled among neighbors or within families with no ill effects, thereby freeing up your time."

And as much as she liked and respected the genie, her restraint finally snapped. She rolled her eyes. "Of course there are. I tell Eastwinders this every day. But until we have some sort of town-wide re-education about behaving like adults who handle their own petty tiffs, I'm obligated to respond to whatever owls come to me. I'm not *permitted* to pass up these types of calls. That's a law this governing body put on the books, and I must abide by it."

Liberty shrugged. "I'll defer to whatever the rest of the Council decides."

While it was refreshing to see the High Council, a notoriously divided body, suddenly come together in a consensus, Bloom felt dangerously close to spreading her wings, flying up to the top of those stupidly tall seats, and smacking each and every member of the High Council on the back of the head. Maybe put a little sense into them. Instead, she forced a pleasant smile.

There *was* one member who hadn't spoken whom she'd hoped would. He was the one who'd convinced her to come today in the first place. But it actually made sense that he would persuade her to do this and then hang her up to dry. That was what a man like him would consider "entertainment."

She was considering thanking them for their time and leaving—maybe she could get a fifteen-minute meditation in if she really hustled—when Count Malavic's voice finally echoed through the chamber.

"For fang's sake. I've never been so embarrassed for each of you in my eternal life." Bloom's heart raced. Did she really have a defender? And could he change anything on his own? "This is our *sheriff*. The woman who keeps this town safe from itself. If we gave her access to the entire treasury and told her to have at it, we still wouldn't be paying her what she deserves. She's our guardian angel in the most literal sense, and you six turn miserly the moment she walks in and asks for a little help in protecting us? Shame on you. As treasurer of this miserable bunch, I say we give her whatever she wants. But I know my vote alone won't do that, so if the rest of you don't unanimously vote to increase her budget to include a deputy, I'll do it out of my own pocket like I did with Fulcrum Park, Veris Bluffs, and the Mancer Academy rebuild. If I remember correctly, I was accused of 'overstepping' all of those times. So, if you wish me not to overstep again, I suggest you give our outstanding sheriff the *pittance* she's demanding."

Nobody spoke right away, but that was all well and good, because he wasn't finished yet. "And why not throw in enough to give the poor woman a proper Sheriff's Office? I stopped by there just the other day and, *damnation*, the place makes my coffin feel spacious. What do you say? Shall we *splurge* on something that actually benefits the town, or would we rather double the Hallow's Faire budget like we did last year and the year before that, and then I'll have to fulfill her requests myself... and take all the credit?"

* * *

Sheriff Bloom remained in a state of shock as she wrapped up a late-night call regarding a garden dispute between two gnomes in the Erin Park neighborhood and set out to complete a specific task she'd been thinking about since her visit to the High Council that morning.

She owed Sebastian Malavic a huge thank you. But how did one thank a vampire who had everything? She'd considered a bottle of wine, except she knew that even with the raise he'd tacked onto her new budget, she couldn't afford one that would compete with the store he kept.

Still unsure what she had to offer him beyond simple spoken gratitude, she dove from the sky and landed on the peninsula in Widow Lake. A short moment later, she knocked on his front door.

Only then did it occur to her what this might look like, arriving at his home so late at night.

He grinned as he answered the door, almost as if he'd been expecting her.

"Hello, Sheriff."

"Count Malavic, I—"

"Sebastian, please."

She restarted. "Sebastian, I just dropped by to—"

"Have a celebratory drink with me? Why, yes, I'd love to. Come on in." He stepped to the side.

"I really don't have the time." But she was already halfway across the threshold, and her resistance held little believability.

"You'll have plenty of time soon, once you hire a deputy," he said, leading her through his well-furnished home into a cozy den. "You can catch up on arresting people later."

"It doesn't work like that."

He shut the door behind her. "You don't say?

Nothing you attend to can wait? Tell me, what was the last call you responded to before coming here?"

Bloom sighed. "Peppep Dippo claimed that Dumdrum Widdle had been stealing mushrooms from his garden for the last week."

"And did you have to arrest the gnome Dumdrum Widdle for... fungal theft?" He motioned to an overstuffed couch by a roaring fire in the cozy lounge where he'd led her, and she took a seat at one end.

"No. It wasn't Dumdrum that was stealing his mushrooms. It was... well, it was a rabbit, obviously."

"Not a were-bunny?"

"No." She couldn't keep the laughter out of her voice now. "A regular old rabbit. I found the entrance to its warren two feet from where the mushrooms had gone missing."

A muscle in the count's jaw twitched as he maintained a straight face, but only just. "That's some fine detective work, Sheriff. The answer was two whole feet away! Almost a yard!" He was standing over her then, staring down, and she found her physical disadvantage here didn't bother her. "How about some wine to celebrate you cracking the case?"

He swooped over to a small rack at the edge of the den and returned with two full wine glasses before she could get her head on straight. She accepted the one he offered her, wondering vaguely if this had the sparkleberry addition like the previous one, and said, "Sebastian, what happened the other night..."

He settled in on the couch beside her. Not on the other end, but right in the middle, leaving little space between them. "What happened the other night?"

"At my office."

He shook his head. "I don't... When I brought you the wine to celebrate your magnificent apprehension of Jacob Pinehorn?"

"You know that's what I'm talking about."

"I do not. Because you referenced something that *happened*, as if it were something deliciously sinful, but nothing happened between us that night."

Trying not to look as rattled as she felt, Bloom sipped her wine. It was a grave mistake. Because riding on the back of the decadent flavors was another decadence, the kind she'd entertained only in her mind, and even then, only in small glimpses. "Nothing happened," she finally managed, "but you know something almost happened. Don't play the fool. We're both adults, and we can admit when we *almost* make a terrible mistake."

Was it just her imagination, or was he leaning closer to her now?

He sipped his wine, never taking his eyes off her. "It wouldn't have been *so* terrible."

"Yes, it would have."

A small, hungry grin emerged on his lips. He cocked his head to the side almost playfully. "There's only one way to be sure." He paused, and the silence hung between them. She hardly dared to move. "Oh! Careful," he said. "You're about to spill your wine." He took the glass from her, setting both it and his own on a table beside the sofa.

"What?" she said, confused. "I wasn't about to—"

"Yes. Yes, you were." He moved with predator skill then, going in for the kill, and, Goddess save her, she met his lips halfway.

Chapter Fifteen

Presently

Gabby Bloom dove out of the night sky, landing silently on the peninsula that stretched out into Widow Lake. She knocked on Count Malavic's front door.

"Hello, Sheriff." He appeared surprised but not altogether unhappy to see her. "I told Ruby it was likely I would have found someone else to preoccupy myself with if she changed her mind and returned to finish what we'd started, but I had no idea it would be *you*. Do I sense a little rivalry? Oh! Don't tell me you're feeling *protective* of me. You devilish angel, after all these years, you're still carrying that torch?"

Sheriff Bloom grinned at him, letting his barbs roll right off her. "Are you finished?"

"I do believe we haven't even gotten start—"

In a blink, she shot out the golden restraints, and the count stared down at his tied wrists, dumbfounded. He looked back up at her. "Oh, so you want it a little rough. For old time's—"

Another golden blaze, and the gag kept him from speaking another word.

That was much better.

"You're under arrest for the murder of Anastasia Vorporal. Why don't you and I take a trip down to that lovely jail you helped build?"

* * *

Count Malavic didn't sulk inside his jail cell like most of the people Bloom arrested. During the hours since his arrest, as he lay on his back on the cot, staring up at the ceiling, he appeared bored but studious, like he was simply passing the time in this new particular way to see how it felt.

Sheriff Bloom watched him through the bars of the cell for a moment more before making her presence known with the creak of the metal door. He rolled his head toward the sound and smirked. "Conjugal visit?"

She ignored him and stuck to her plan. "Ruby believes that if you did kill Anastasia Vorporal, it was for a good reason. Is that true?"

He sat up and threw his legs over the side of the cot. "I've never met someone named Anastasia… *Whoever* in my life."

Bloom shrugged and approached, stopping only a few feet shy of him. She stared down at where he sat. She had all the power here. Yes, she much preferred this dynamic when dealing with the vampire. "Fair enough. Perhaps you knew her by another name." She pulled from her breast pocket a picture and held it out. It was of the body of Anastasia on the floor of Veris Bluffs Asylum.

The count took it from her and brought it close to his face, inspecting it closely. "That's definitely a vampire, but no, I still don't recognize her."

More than ever, Bloom wished her Judgment would work against him to help her guess if he were lying. His expression showed no signs that he was.

But she wasn't at a dead end yet.

She took the photo from him and switched it out with the other one in her pocket. "What about her? Do you recognize her at all?"

The moment the count laid eyes on the image of Sophia Gerards, his lips parted, and Bloom thought she heard a slight, involuntary intake of air. His nostrils twitched and his eyebrows pinched as he gazed intently at the image he now held.

Then he handed the second photo back to the sheriff. "No. I'm afraid I haven't a clue who she is, either. Was she found dead as well?"

"You really have never seen that girl in your life?"

"I've really never seen her. She looks awful, though. Sickly. What kind of creature is she?"

"A waif." Bloom fretted as she tucked the photograph away again. "Well, something called a Skarbnik, but then also a waif."

"Fascinating," he said, not sounding the least bit fascinated. "Anything else you want to ask me? Perhaps where I was at the time of the murder? I'm afraid you might not like the answer..."

* * *

Ruby True's mind was in a knotty twist. She should have been asleep hours ago, but sleep wouldn't come. What a strange day she'd had, even by her standards.

She rolled over in bed to stare off the side. "Clifford? You awake?"

"Sure am. Can't sleep."

"Yeah, me neither," she whispered. Her house was too silent, for one. Her bedroom and bathroom took up the entire second story of the narrow three-story cottage. And while the open parlor, kitchen, and a small guest bathroom were well lived in on the first floor, there was still the matter of the empty third story that contributed greatly to her growing awareness that she was nearing fifty and lived entirely alone (outside of her familiar).

Having more house than one needs could do that. Maybe someday she could rent it out, if she could ever find someone brave enough to rent from a Fifth Wind witch. Most people weren't looking to live somewhere with high spiritual traffic, and while the bottom two stories were well warded against anything dark, she did still have unexpected ghostly visitors. It was how she paid the bills, after all. Help a spirit out, collect a little from the loved ones.

But tonight, there were no spirits at her window or bedside. It was just her, Clifford, and all her thoughts.

"I imagine you're a little disappointed in me."

"What for? That moment in the treasury?"

"The one with Sebastian, yes."

Clifford got up from his soft bed and approached the edge of her mattress, resting his large head on the quilt beside her. *"I'm not disappointed at all. It wasn't easy seeing Zax with Filaemenia at the tearoom this morning.*

Sure, I wasn't exactly eager to bear witness to you and the count's encounter, but I looked away and thought of something else while it happened." He licked her hand once. *"But no, not at all disappointed. I was a little glad, actually."*

"Glad?" Ruby asked, stroking one of Clifford's ears.

"Yes. The last time you were sad for this same reason, you ended up in the count's arms and it helped you feel a little less sad for a while. I thought the same thing might happen this time."

"Oh, Cliff. You're such a sweet soul." She kissed him on the forehead, and, already feeling better, was sure she could get some sleep now.

Then the banging began at her front door.

Chapter Sixteen

Clifford stood at the ready as Ruby, now covered in a fleece robe, opened the front door to see who in the hellhound was trying to bang it down at this time of night.

"Hi, Ruby. Did I wake you up? Heh."

"Death waits for no one," she mumbled. "What can I help you with, Ted?"

"I need your help. I was supposed to meet Count Malavic at Sheehan's tonight for a few rounds of scufflepuck, but he never showed. I sent an owl to him as a reminder and never heard back. I can't seem to find him."

Ruby's eyebrows rose at the reaper darkening her doorstep in the dead of night. "Are you worried about him?"

"Of course! This isn't like him. And considering there was that murdered vampire in Veris Bluffs, well, it sure seems suspicious. I thought you might know something about it."

"I do," she said, pulling her robe tighter against the chill from outside. "You're not far off on the two events being related. Count Malavic was the one who murdered Anastasia Vorporal in Veris Bluffs Asylum this morning. He didn't show up to Sheehan's Pub because Sheriff Bloom has already arrested him."

Ted's creaky voice broke as he shouted, "What?!"

The outrage came as a bit of a shock, and she shared a quick surprised glance with her familiar. "Are you so surprised that Malavic had it in him to murder another vampire?"

"No, definitely not. It's just that I was with him all morning."

"Oh dear." Ruby stepped to the side. "You'd better come in and tell me."

Ted stayed put. "It's not that long a tale. Last night, we stayed at Sheehan's until it closed, and then he came back to my cabin in the Deadwoods to keep drinking. I've been distilling warwillow root from the Murderswamp for the last few months, and the batch was finally ready to sample. Well, if you know anything about warwillow root liquor, you know it will knock you right onto your backside. He ended up staying with me all night. And since I don't sleep, it wasn't like he could have slipped out when I wasn't paying attention. When he woke up the next morning, I accompanied him on a bit of a hunt in the Deadwoods—nothing sentient, just a few jackalopes—and once he was replenished, I was just absolutely craving one of Harley Hardtime's meat pies, so he and I went over to A New Leaf, and that's where I left him."

Ruby frowned. "And that's where I found him."

"You did? Perfect! What time did he leave A New Leaf?"

She considered it. "About nine fifteen." She frowned. "That's plenty of time for him to make it over to the asylum to murder the other vampire."

But Ted only shook his head victoriously. "Except he *didn't* have that time because I met him back at Sheehan's at half past nine!"

"Good goddess," Ruby said, "do you men never stop drinking?"

"Guess not. Heh. But to be fair, I can't get drunk. I just like the taste. Don't you see, though? Between you and me, Sebastian never had the opportunity to make it to Veris Bluffs for the murder!"

Ruby allowed herself a moment to ponder. "And you're sure he didn't leave your sight?"

Ted shook his head, sending ripples through the dark hood that obscured his face. "He stepped outside the pub for a moment to send an owl, but that's it."

"An owl?"

"Said it was High Council business he'd forgotten about. On account of the distilled warwillow we'd had the night before."

"Ah."

"See?" Ted continued. "There's no way he could have murdered her!"

"Fangs and claws," she muttered. "But the spirit of Anastasia told me it was him."

Ted shrugged. "Ghosts can lie too."

"Indeed, but why would she?"

"Beats me. Heh. Will you go down to the station with mc to speak with the sheriff?"

Ruby was tempted to ask if it could wait until morning, which she knew it could, but she quickly concluded that there was little chance of her going back to sleep after this new puzzling revelation, so she accepted her sleepless fate and instead replied, "Yes. Let me get dressed."

* * *

Sheriff Bloom looked as confused as Ruby felt once Ted had finished relaying Malavic's alibi in her private office.

"But the spirit..." Bloom began.

"I know, I know," Ruby said, waving it off. "She must have lied, and I don't know why. I shouldn't have believed her at face value. Most spirits are fairly truthful because they have little else to lose. Yes, they do omit things here and there to preserve their sense of identity, but rarely do they outright lie and try to get the wrong person convicted for their murder! I should have known something was off, though. The fact that a vampire even *has* a spirit is suspect to begin with."

Bloom nodded. "Can you summon her now?"

"I can certainly try. But I suspect she exists outside the usual spiritual plane." Ruby settled into the chair in the corner of the office and shut her eyes, letting her mind relax until she found herself in the In-Between place. It looked much like the park where she used to spend her more peaceful moments before coming to Eastwind.

Ruby sat on a wooden bench. There was the pristine lake ahead of her, and between her and it, a busy walking path. Of course, she knew that the people who passed her and lounged on the green grass around her were not her imagination, nor were they living people. They were spirits who inhabited the In-Between. This was where she could call to them, speak to them in a more relaxed setting, and seek out any who might be lingering in the area but not visible to her naked eye in Eastwind.

She called to Anastasia and waited for a response, but even as she did, she knew one wouldn't come.

Ruby opened her eyes to Bloom's office again. "No. She's not there, and I suspect she wouldn't want to be found anyway. She seems to function very much on her own terms."

"Not much to do about that, then. Perhaps don't trust her again," Bloom suggested.

"Wasn't planning on it."

The sheriff turned to Ted. "I'd like for you to tell me what you know of the body. I should have the medical examiner's report in tomorrow and the magical examiner's a day or two later, but you usually get a solid read on the state of the corpse. Someone murdered the vampire Anastasia, and if it wasn't Malavic, then we have a killer on the loose." She stood and approached Ruby. "While Ted and I discuss this, Ruby, I have a special task for you."

She led Ruby and Clifford out of her office for a private word, and once they were in the hallway said, "I don't believe Malavic's hands are entirely clean here."

Ruby felt her ears perk up then realized she was merely feeling that vicariously from her familiar. "But he has an alibi."

"And you and I both know that means nothing as far as being involved. He might not have driven the stake through the woman, but I just have this feeling he knows more about it than he's letting on. Don't you?"

Ruby frowned. "Yes. My Insight was niggling me about that same thing the whole walk over with Ted."

"Great, then I need you to do me a huge favor."

Ruby eyed the sheriff closely, already guessing she wouldn't like this favor one bit.

"I need you to dig deeper with him for me."

"And in what reality would Malavic want to tell me anything useful after I turned him in on suspicion of murder?" Bloom's gaze became intense and full of heat, and Ruby broke eye contact when she realized what was going on. "Oh, don't you dare look into my soul like that, you Peeping Tom! Just ask me straight out what you're looking for."

The sheriff suppressed a grin. "I don't need to ask. I already know. You and dear old Sebastian were on the precipice of something in the treasury before the spirit dropped in, weren't you?"

Ruby felt her face flush. "I don't—"

"Not judging."

"That's a change."

"You know I *can't* judge on this one," Bloom said on a sigh. "I have no room to. And I'm not mentioning it to put you on the spot, Ruby. I'm only mentioning it because I believe that it gives you a solid explanation for *why* you would want to apologize to him, to make nice. And then you *extract information from him*."

Ruby straightened up. "You want me to cozy up to the count to pump him for information."

The angel grinned. "Yes. Is that going to be a problem?"

Ruby nibbled on her bottom lip, considering. "No, I think that might be all right."

"Wait. That's not going to cause a problem between you and Zax if it gets out that you're spending time with Sebastian, will it?"

The Fifth Wind sighed heavily. "No, that will be no problem at all."

Bloom leaned forward, placing a gentle hand on Ruby's shoulder. "When we get this thing figured out, how about tea at your house, and you can tell me all about *that*."

"Not much to tell, but I'll never turn down casual time with the town's most in-demand woman."

"Then it's a date. But in the meantime, and I don't mean this as an insult, you look tired. Go get some sleep. I'll handle the release of Malavic once I finish up with Ted. When you wake up, send word for him to meet you for dinner somewhere nice."

"It needs to be somewhere nice?"

"It doesn't need to be, but you might as well milk a delicious dinner out of it."

"I wouldn't let him pay! Then it would be like a real date."

Bloom rolled her eyes. "Fine. Miss a delicious meal if you must. But go rest, give him a few hours to think things over, and then send word his way that you'd like to apologize for getting him arrested."

"You think he'll accept?"

"I know he will. Don't forget, the count's biggest enemy isn't you or me, it's boredom. A dinner with the witch who almost put him away for murder will be intriguing enough that he could never turn it down."

Chapter Seventeen

There was a bitter part of Ruby she didn't usually indulge that rejoiced at the idea of meeting Count Malavic for dinner at this particular place.

After her initial correspondence with him, it was he who'd suggested the restaurant at Treetop Lodge to pick up where they left off in the treasury, and she'd known *exactly* why he'd suggested it. Yes, the steaks were excellent, but his reasoning, she was sure, had little to do with the food, and more to do with who they were likely to encounter while there.

She was fully rested now, after a full night's sleep over the course of the morning and early afternoon. Sure, she'd had a few dreams that had caused her heart to race in anticipation of this meeting, but those were by no means nightmares. Quite the contrary.

She'd arrived at the restaurant on Fluke Mountain a few minutes early and wasn't concerned when she was the first one there. The count arrived right on time, and she watched as he spoke with the hostess and motioned that he was meeting someone.

Me, she thought. *He's here to meet me.* The fact that any somewhat handsome man wanted to meet her was a small but welcome ego boost. Sometimes one needed a morsel like that, especially when one was aging faster than one's joints and back could keep up.

Malavic slid into his chair across the small table from her. She'd requested one at the back with a large window overlooking the lake. It was hard not to feel a bit of excitement when a view of such great awe was near at hand.

At least that's what Ruby told herself was the reason she felt her heart race and stomach flutter when Sebastian reached across the table, took her hand, and kissed it.

She opened her mouth to speak, but before she could, he said, "I forgive you."

"Oh." She blinked. "And here I was with this big speech on why I didn't deserve it but hoped you would consider such a thing anyway."

He grabbed his cloth napkin from the table, shook it out, and set it delicately across his lap. "No need. From what I glean, you were told directly that I was the guilty party from what one generally assumes to be a credible source. But it does raise three serious questions."

"And those are?"

"First, how in the world did a vampire communicate with you via the spiritual plane when it's well documented that my kind does not have a spirit to outlast us? Second, why on earth would she lie and say I murdered her when I clearly did not? And lastly, would you like to split a bottle of wine with me, or are you more in the mood for beer?"

"Depends on who's paying," she said.

"Oh, you are, of course. You were the one who invited me out."

She jerked her head back. "Well, I suppose you're right. But you're the one who suggested this restaurant. We could have picked somewhere cheaper."

"I didn't suggest it because of the price, as I think you know. I suggested it because of *that*." He nodded toward the host stand, and she turned to see that Zax Banderfield had just arrived for his nightly meal. It was no secret the werebear frequented this place on a daily basis. One of the perks of being the head of the werebear sleuth was that he could eat here for free (though Ruby knew he always left a hefty tip when the waitstaff or owner truly refused to let him pay).

"Ooh, too bad," Malavic said. "Doesn't look like he has company tonight. Perhaps Filaemenia stood him up. Shall I invite him over?"

"Don't you dare," Ruby snapped. Then she regained herself. "Perhaps he just wants to have a meal alone. Nothing wrong with that."

"Nothing at all. And it will make it so much easier to drive him mad with jealousy." He reached out and took her hand again, holding it firmly until she felt Zax's eyes on them, at which point the count brought her hand up to his lips again, taking his sweet time.

"Really," she scolded him, but she didn't pull her hand away, and grinned despite herself.

He looked up at her, his mouth still only an inch away from her skin. "You seem to be enjoying this."

"Nothing about you brings out the best in me, that's for sure."

"My dear witch, you have to let your darker nature out to play *sometime*. Might as well be around someone who will appreciate it rather than judge you for it."

When the server approached, Malavic went ahead and ordered a bottle of wine that Ruby had never heard of. She searched the wine list and found it listed at the bottom. It was the only one with no price listed next to it.

"Sweet baby jackalope," she muttered.

"What is it?" he said.

She shot him a quick glare. "Didn't anyone teach you that if someone else is buying, you don't pick the most expensive thing on the menu?"

"No. No one taught me any such thing, but if it's out of your price range, all you need to do is say so, and I'll pay for this lovely dinner of ours myself. However, that will mean that it's no longer an apology but rather a date."

"We're not on a date."

"Then you're paying?"

"We're not on a date, but you're paying."

He leaned forward, elbows on the table, fists under his chin. He looked both haunting and charming in the flickering light of the candle between them. "Why are you so resistant to this being a date? I've already told you I won't grow attached. I could never love a mortal. If you grow tired of me, all you need do is say so, and I'll happily find my next diversion."

"You only started pursuing me when you realized Zax had found someone else. I don't need anyone's pity."

"It's not pity. Yes, I'm an opportunist, no denying

that. It was merely the case of finding an in with you again. I've been waiting, but I knew that if I tried before you were well shook of that great hairy oaf, I would be doing no one any favors. Encroaching on you while he still felt he had a claim would only have resulted in an attempt on his part to stake that claim more strongly, and if anything, it would have kept you two together longer for no reason at all. Not to mention, it would have created some unwanted conflict within the High Council."

"No conflict is unwanted by you," she said.

"I do love to stir the cauldron, as you witches say, but I *never* need the inconvenience of a werebear trying to act tough to protect his ego. It gets in the way of me doing whatever I please."

Ruby snuck another glance Zax's way and saw that he'd intentionally sat so that his back was to her and Malavic. She felt a small stabbing pain in her chest. Did he not care about her that much? Did it not affect him to see her out with another man, like it had affected her to see him out with another woman?

Instinctively, she reached under the table for the soft, reassuring touch of Clifford's head, then remembered he'd agreed to stay home and continue snoozing by the fire at her suggestion.

"I can feel it, you know," Sebastian said, "your loneliness."

She shot him a sharp look. "I have no idea what you mean."

But the vampire remained undeterred. "It's just something I can do. Part of being who I am. I can feel the pain of others, and it pulls me in, attracts me. I suppose it's a survival instinct for my kind. We need people to let us in before we can drink from them with their consent, and those who are hurting and lonely are much more likely to let the wrong person in."

"You're exploiting me. You're a predator."

"I am a predator; I don't think I've ever denied that. But I won't drink from you if that's what concerns you. And is it really 'exploitation' if you're getting something you need from time spent with me?"

"What do you presume I'm getting out of this?"

"Companionship, reassurance, knowing you're wanted. And I want you, Ruby True, I think that's plain enough. It's symbiotic between us. Is it so terrible that I'm attracted to your pain if I help to ease it?"

"I don't believe it," she said. "You can't feel anyone's pain because you're incapable of feeling it yourself."

The count cocked his head to the side. "Is that what you think? That I've never experienced it myself?"

She wanted to say yes, but something held her back.

"I have," he said. "I've experienced soul-crushing pain, loss like you can't even imagine, and loneliness without end. I wasn't always like this. I was mortal once. And then everything was taken from me—my life, my death, as well as my soul. *That* is pain I hope you never have to experience. I had a future once. And now I have nothing but eternity."

Ruby was spared finding the right words to say by the waitress approaching and dropping off the wine. "Are you ready to order?"

"I'll have the tenderloin rare, no sides, and she'll have the same but medium rare and with the whipped truffle potatoes and roasted broccolini."

Ruby would have been upset by the count's

presumption of ordering for her if he hadn't picked out the exact thing she'd been eyeing on the menu before he'd arrived. So instead, she contented herself with nitpicking. "I prefer it cooked medium."

"Not once you taste it medium rare." He filled each of their wine glasses. "What were we talking about? Actually, it doesn't matter." He held up his glass. "Here's to our first real date. May we both bury our pain in a landslide of pleasure."

Her stomach fluttered again, and she told herself it was merely from hunger. She raised her glass as well. "I won't go *that* far, but I will toast to companionship."

"I'll take whatever I can get," Malavic said, "for now."

Chapter Eighteen

The only way Ruby was able to justify being in Count Malavic's home after what had turned out to be a lovely and delicious dinner together at Treetop Lodge was that this was part of the investigation.

Unfortunately, once she had begun to fill herself with delicious wine and steak, her ability to do the one thing Sheriff Bloom asked of her, to pump Malavic for some useful information regarding the murder, had vanished entirely.

It was late now. They'd stayed drinking and talking in the restaurant much longer than she could ever remember having done on a date—

No, not a date.

— before, and Zax Banderfield had long since left by the time Sebastian had asked for the check and paid with a handful of gold coins without so much as looking at the total due. Having overpaid by tenfold, he then took Ruby's arm and led her from the restaurant before their waitress could even attempt to make change.

"I want to show you something." They stood in the entry hall of his castle now, having just arrived. He took her coat from her, hanging it up in the closet.

"What is it you want to show me?"

"Something that might change your mind about me."

She scoffed lightly, enjoying the carefree feeling the wine had left her with. "You presume to have a clue where my mind stands on you presently."

He shot her a skeptical look and then motioned to the grand staircase ahead. "It's upstairs."

"If this is your way of getting me to your bedroom, I'll be greatly disappointed. I expected you to be slicker than this." But she followed him up the stairs just the same.

Where he led her wasn't a bedroom, but a library. Candles on wall sconces burst into flame the moment they entered, illuminating the long rows of books... and other objects of interest. Pictures, keepsakes under glass, preserved specimens of animals Ruby had never seen before in her life, nor even heard about roaming the Deadwoods— the whole place seemed like it belonged in another world, and she began to suspect that might actually be the case.

Malavic strode over to a portrait on the wall, examining it with such a warm intensity Ruby had no choice but to stand beside him and take it in. "That's you, isn't it?" She almost didn't recognize him in it, despite his main features being an unmistakable match. But the man posing for the portrait might as well have lived an entirely different life.

That was the thing about portraits, Ruby mused. The brilliant ones captured not the outside but the inside of a man, and this one had done exactly that.

She stepped closer. The Sebastian Malavic of the portrait had skin the color of honey, not the unsaturated hue of the man standing beside her. But that wasn't the biggest difference between the two versions. Neither was the fact that the portrait depicted a man who appeared to be a decade younger than the Sebastian she'd always known.

No, the greatest difference was something else. An essence that exuded from this young man. Could it be? Was she sensing through this work of art the very soul that was now missing?

"I sat for this portrait twelve years before I was turned." His rich voice sent a shiver down her spine. When she looked up at him, it felt like seeing a ghost, just the essence of the man that once was, doomed to wander the earth knowing what part of himself he'd lost but never able to reclaim it. He was a spirit with unfinished business. But no, he was the opposite of that: spiritless with no business left to attend to.

"Is all of this from your old life?" she asked.

"And my old world, yes. I couldn't bear to live in the same place where all of my prior years were spent. I wanted to preserve those memories, yes, but not taint them with my new reality. And so I packed up what I could to remind me—I knew even then how much I would need a reminder of who I was—and found a new home. One where I would be the only vampire around, where I couldn't be easily tainted by the baser impulses of my kind, where I wouldn't learn to accept and justify them. I could decide for myself what it was to be vampire, build my own rules, my own morals and ethics.

Mortal codes no longer applied to me, but I refused to live by the vampire code."

Another small sketch of him caught her attention on a wooden side table, and she brought it up closer to inspect. It was surprisingly detailed for the charcoal used, and it showed him smiling.

In fact, he was smiling *at* someone. But the edge of the drawing had been torn, and the object of Sebastian's affection was gone. He didn't wish to remember *all* parts of his old life, it seemed.

"Who were you before you were turned?" she asked.

His side pressed up against hers, and he slipped an arm around her waist as he gazed down at the drawing in her hand. "I was a simple man. I was in love. Desperately in love. We were going to start a family. I could see the rest of my life spread out before of me. I could even see beyond my life, to the generations of life my love would spawn."

"The other half of this drawing..." She let the question finish itself.

"Ah, sometimes it hurts too much to remember the things we can't get back. Not all reminders of the past are happy ones at present, and often the happiest times of the past cause the most agony. Besides, I can see her whenever I want." He shut his eyes, and Ruby understood.

This woman, the one he'd fallen madly in love with, was like his own version of Ruby's In-Between place. The mystery woman had brought peace and solace to his heart —all he had to do was close his eyes and she appeared.

Had Ruby ever experienced a love like that? Would she?

"You had to leave her," she said, her heart breaking for him.

He grabbed the sketch from her hand and tossed it, turning her to face him. "It takes everything in me not to turn around and do to others what my sire did to me. To *take* from them what was taken from me. To spread my misery far and wide. I'm drawn to pain because I can't suffer happiness. It's no longer within my reach through no fault of my own. I suffer, and I want others to suffer with me. It's the only companionship I can tolerate." He pulled her closer, his voice hardly more than a hoarse whisper. "Despite my misery, I want to create more of it. It's a thirst far stronger than my thirst for blood. Where my soul once was now exists a pit. I am a monster, and I want to create more of my kind. I've lost everything and now I want to take away what others have."

Ruby stared into his eyes and found his pupils large, his eyes glistening with emotion. And she found she wasn't afraid. "Do you want to take away everything I have, Sebastian? Do you want to make a monster of me?"

"No, my dear witch. But I do want other things from you right now. Those who are suffering are my only respite. I hope to ease your suffering, if only briefly."

She pressed herself closer to the vampire. "And how do you imagine you'll ease my suffering, Sebastian?"

"The more important question is this: How do *you* imagine it?" His lips crashed into hers, and she wound her arms around his neck, giving herself this one moment, this rest from the loneliness and heartbreak, from control and propriety and the confines of decency.

Just one night, that was all.

Chapter Nineteen

✾✾✾

9 years before the present

Ruby True was starving, but that wasn't her most pressing concern that morning when she woke up in Count Malavic's bed alone.

How had she let this happen? A night with the count?

And what a night it was.

"Not the point!" she hissed at herself.

And yet, when she groped around inside her for feelings of shame, she found... none. *Huh.*

It was a delightful surprise. Maybe she was under no obligation to feel guilty or ashamed for going home with Sebastian after their enjoyable time at Sheehan's Pub. It had certainly taken her mind off Ezra Ares. And besides, she was a grown woman! She could find her diversions as she pleased, and who had the right to tell her not to?

And yet, this could obviously *never* happen again.

Once dressed, Ruby tiptoed out of the bedroom and

down the stairs toward the front door. Was the count at home, or had he already gone out? Was he sleeping in his coffin? Either way, best to just slip out without being seen.

She opened the front door just enough to squeeze through, then shut it as quietly as she could behind her.

"Have fun?" Clifford yawned from his place on the front step and stretched his front paws, sticking his rear into the air.

"You didn't have to wait for me," she said.

"Yes, I did. This first time, at least. Had to make sure it wasn't just a trap for him to drink you."

"First time? Last time, you mean."

Clifford got to his feet, leaning forward to stretch his hips. *"If you insist. No judgement from me. I enjoyed listening to the water lap against the peninsula all night."*

She scratched his head. *"I'm sorry you were left alone in this cold all night. You probably could have used some company, too."*

"It was nice to be alone out here, actually. Gave me time to collect my thoughts."

Ruby patted at her hair, wondering what sort of wild shape it held. *"I could do with a little time to collect my thoughts, I think."*

"How about a stop by the library then a visit to A New Leaf?" the hellhound suggested.

"Yes, but add in a stop by home first to get myself together."

She cast one final look at the count's castle and thought, *That was nice, but never again. That's a promise.*

Chapter Twenty

109 years before the present

Sheriff Gabby Bloom snapped out of her deep meditative state with a start. Where was she? Her bedroom looked nothing like this.

Oh no.

What time was it? Had she missed emergency owls in the meantime? Had the owls flown to the castle only to be turned away? Had Eastwind been left unprotected for—

How long had she been meditating? Goddess knew she was overdue for a long spell of it, so it might have been hours and hours. Could it have been *days*? Oh, Heaven above!

She sat up in bed and looked down at herself. She seemed to have lost her mind the night before, but at least she'd had the awareness to put her clothes back on. But something was missing...

She spotted her badge on the side table, and swung

her feet around, snatching it up. Her boots were set out by the side of the bed as well, but that could wait. There was a piece of parchment beneath where her badge had been. She picked it up and read it.

I hope you'll come back the next time you need a break from the stress of work. Last night was heavenly.
-S

"Sweet harp's song," Bloom swore under her breath, and then she shoved her feet into her boots and crept down the stairs and out the front door.

She was relieved to realize that it was only just dawn. So long as she hadn't meditated straight through entire days, she'd only been out of commission for a few hours. Small blessings.

The sheriff began down the path away from the castle, lost in her thoughts, but paused and looked back over her shoulder.

This could never happen again, she told herself. It was a one-time thing. An angel had *no* business mingling with a vampire, never mind the fact that she was the sheriff and he was on the High Council.

She was just about to turn around and fly back to her cramped office when she realized she was clutching something in her hand. Funny, since she hadn't remembered grabbing anything. She held it out and saw that it was Sebastian's note from the bedside table. She'd taken it with her without thinking. Her eyes scanned over the last words. *Last night was heavenly.*

It was, wasn't it, she thought, and a small grin fought its way to her lips.

Perhaps no owls at all had come for her during her rendezvous. Or perhaps if any had, they were for silly things that neighbors ought to learn to handle amongst themselves...

Could she spare a few more hours? Could she go wake him from his coffin for—

No, you silly woman! One time is acceptable. Everyone makes mistakes. It might have been a lovely one, but it was still a mistake all the same!

The angel looked down at the note again, considered tossing it into the lake, but instead slipped it into the breast pocket of her uniform before taking to the sky and flying back to her lonely, cramped office.

Chapter Twenty-One

Presently

Ruby knew exactly where she was when she woke up the next morning. She'd been there before, much to her chagrin.

And I promised never again.

Was she upset with herself? She couldn't be sure. Perhaps she only felt she *ought* to be upset with herself, because nothing her six senses were experiencing told her this was a bad place to be. The mattress was soft, the comforter was warm, and there was a rich floral scent filling the air of Sebastian Malavic's bedroom.

Roses? She sat up and looked around, quickly locating the vase of midnight black roses upon the bedside table. Her favorite color, too.

Beside the flowers was a note. She picked it up.

Thank you for the delicious diversion. Come back any time you need another.

-S

A shiver ran down her spine, though whether that was from the chilly air of the room or a vivid image from the night before was entirely unclear.

While she considered lying back down and waiting to see if the count returned to check on her, she remembered that there were more pressing matters that demanded her attention.

Murder, for instance.

She hadn't gotten any of the information she might have liked from him. She'd gotten plenty of other things she liked very much, but nothing she could take back to Bloom.

"Fangs and claws."

Once dressed, she slipped out through the front door. No Clifford waiting for her this time.

She started down the narrow peninsula on her own but paused and looked back at the castle. This really, *truly* had to be the last time.

Or perhaps the last time until someone else breaks my heart.

Sebastian really *was* a fantastic salve upon that wound. Perhaps he was more of a philanthropist than she'd given him credit for.

She allowed herself yet another indulgence of recounting the events of the previous evening as she strolled down the strip of land leading away from the castle.

It was still early morning and bitterly cold, but she hardly felt the chill. Her recent memories were keeping her nice and warm.

She made it to the shore and hardly farther when she collided with someone emerging from a wooded path that forked into hers. "Oh! Sorry," she said. She blinked, pulled herself from her thoughts, and glanced at whomever she'd just absentmindedly collided with.

The air caught in her lungs.

"Ruby," Zax said stiffly. "You're up early."

She scrambled for something to say as his eyes followed the path she must have just walked... straight from the castle.

"Huh," he said, his expression like a stone wall.

"I just had to pay him an early morning visit. Official business."

"Was it related to the business I saw the two of you discussing at the restaurant last night?"

"There was a murder," she blurted. "A vampire was murdered."

He showed no sign of interest, nor particularly of believing her. "Ah. So you've decided to go undercover to extract information from him, then? I'm sure you've made it very *believable*."

"Yes, I'm very sly. But I didn't know you were also doing consulting for Sheriff Bloom."

His brows pinched, and a deep crease appeared above the bridge of his strong nose.

Ruby went on, "Or is there *another* reason you're taking Filaemenia to what you *know* to be my favorite tearoom at a time when you *know* I'm likely to be there?"

She didn't think it was possible for him to stand any straighter than he was, but suddenly he did. "I'm not sure where you get off passing judgments on who I spend time with, Ruby. Not after how much effort I put into trying to spend time with you."

"Pah," she said. "You only tried in the hours you already had free. It wasn't as if you were skipping days of work to come see me in *my* free hours."

"I have a sleuth to lead. I'm on the High Council. I don't have the luxury of flexibility that you do."

She tilted her chin upward. "My flexibility is no longer any of your concern."

"Clearly," he said. "I see you're saving all your flexibility for my dear friend the count."

Her mouth fell open. "The presumptions! At least I have flexibility to begin with. I'm done doing all the work for any man, Zax. There's no point in discussing it further. We both gave up on this a while ago. I hope you enjoy that elf's flexibility while you can. A long-lifer like her will be done with you soon."

"Says the woman who just left the bed of an immortal!" he called after her as she hurried down the path.

She wouldn't dignify that with a response. Instead, she called over her shoulder. "Please don't follow me, Zax. I'd like a little peace and quiet on my walk home after such a busy night."

There. That one would sting. Or at least she hoped it would. She refused to turn around to check. She wouldn't give him that satisfaction.

Ruby was feeling well and pleased with herself as she continued down the rocky path into town until she heard footsteps approaching her quickly from behind.

Yes! she thought as her heart leapt. *He's chasing me down. He won't let me leave. We can forget all about our conflicting schedules and our stubbornness and find a way to make it work!*

She turned, searching for the werebear's face, those soft lips, his warm body that she would lean into and that would shield her against the cold.

But instead, she found a boy in the early throes of puberty, panting and out of breath.

"Stu," she said, "are you okay? Is someone chasing you?"

"Miss True," he said between pants. "The sheriff sent me to find you."

Ruby looked around. "She sent you to find me *here*?"

He nodded. "She said you might be on your way back to town after early morning business with Count Malavic."

"*Did* she?"

"She needs you to come with me right away."

Stu Manchester, though not yet to his growth spurt, was already nearly as tall as she was, though that wasn't saying much for someone of her short stature. She eyed the young were-elk closely. "What for? Where are we going?"

"Veris Bluffs," the boy said. "There's been a development. She needs your gifts."

Ruby nodded. "Veris Bluffs is no place for a boy your age, Stu. I know my way. You head on into town."

"Yes, ma'am."

"Wait." She reached in her pocket and pulled out a copper coin. "Get yourself a slice of warm pie somewhere."

His eyes lit up. "Thank you, Miss True. I love pie!"

"You've earned a slice for your hard work. Off you go."

Sweet baby jackalope, she thought, heading back the way she'd just come, *that kid needs to get some friends.*

As Ruby made for Veris Bluffs, she spared a quick glance toward the tree-covered path where Zax had emerged from moments ago but found it empty. He'd listened to her request, then, and not followed.

She sighed. She could hardly be mad at a man for respecting her wishes.

Then she took the forested path in opposite direction, the one that would lead around the lake and out to Veris Bluffs Asylum, where who-knew-what was awaiting her.

Chapter Twenty-Two

Sheriff Bloom greeted Ruby outside The Bad Side entrance and shoved a croissant her way. The angel smiled smugly. "Figured you might not have had a chance to grab breakfast."

Ruby gladly accepted the offering. "I can't imagine why you would presume such a thing." She tore the croissant down the middle and shoved half of it in her mouth at once.

"You might not want to eat *too* much just yet."

"Ah aaht?" Ruby said, and when the angel arched a brow at her, she finished chewing and tried again. "That bad in there?"

Bloom shook her head slowly. "Not good, that's for sure. Interesting, but not pleasant."

Sheriff Bloom offered Ruby a handkerchief from her pocket, and the Fifth Wind took it with a grateful nod, wrapping it around the flakey pastry and tucking the bundle in her coat pocket. Then the angel led the way inside.

While the prison-like structure did a good job of shielding Ruby from the cruel wind, she sensed little improvement in temperature as she followed the sheriff down the long, stark hallway until they reached the familiar turnoff to Sophia Gerards's cell. "In here," said Bloom, holding open the door.

Ruby stepped inside and saw immediately why the sheriff had summoned her so urgently. And also why Bloom had warned her against eating too much.

Three words appeared to be finger-painted across the wall over the waif's bed, and Ruby only needed only one guess at what substance was used to create such dark red ink.

Ruby read the three words over and over again. What did they mean? Clearly, they were significant. She couldn't imagine *anyone*, no matter the mental state, going to this much effort to write a sentence that didn't hold some personal significance.

"Get any read off them?" Bloom asked.

Ruby had. Her Insight had practically screamed a few key points at her as soon is she'd entered this space and laid eyes on the writing. Unfortunately, the *why* of it all wasn't among the screaming. "Only whose hand wrote them. And whose blood was used." She nodded toward the bed. Upon the covers, the waif lie curled in a fetal pose with Head Healer Ryker sitting beside her, gently stroking the girl's hair.

The waif's eyes were open wide, but it was clear she wasn't seeing anything in the physical world around her. The white sheets of her bed and the edge of her pillow that she clutched with one hand were stained crimson.

She was alive, though. The bleeding had been stemmed one way or another.

"She's been lying there since they came to deliver her breakfast and discovered the writing an hour ago," Bloom said.

But Ruby hardly heard it. Instead, her attention had locked onto the object the waif held to her stomach. The stuffed toy. Head Healer Ryker had made good on her word, it seemed, and sewn up the hellhound quickly.

Ruby suddenly longed for her familiar, the soft touch of his fur. She would send for Clifford by owl before she left. She wasn't ready to go home to her quiet house just yet, but she desperately needed tea. And Bloom would want to discuss this new development, no doubt.

"She won't speak to anyone," Bloom said, though it could have gone unsaid. That the waif was catatonic was clear enough. "Any idea of the *meaning* behind the words?"

"I certainly have a guess, and I assume you do as well." Ruby chewed her bottom lip. "But I'll need some tea before we work through our suspicions."

The sheriff nodded and motioned for Ruby to proceed ahead of her out of the cell.

But before she did, Ruby gave the scrawled writing another hard look. Just three words could unlock a world of understanding if the meaning of them could be confirmed.

The waif had sent her message loud and clear: *BRING IT BACK.*

Chapter Twenty-Three

109 years before the present

Sheriff Bloom was a woman on a mission as she landed down the road from Sheehan's Pub and walked the rest of the way.

In her spare moments between arrests and paperwork over the last week, she'd deliberated about taking this action and had finally come to a decision.

The count would be drinking inside, she knew. She'd flown there just for him.

It was rarely a comforting sight for any of Sheehan's patrons when the town's sheriff entered the pub in full uniform, so she wasn't expecting a warm welcome.

But only after she pulled open the heavy door and stepped inside the dusty spot did she remember that it was a weekend night.

The place was packed, and all activity ceased in a ripple away from her as soon as she crossed the threshold.

She maintained her composure. She had nothing to

worry about from any of these people. That wasn't how the power flowed. But how many of them thought they had something to fear from her? How many petty crimes had she just interrupted upon arrival?

It didn't matter. Not tonight. She wasn't here for petty crime.

She scanned the room, feeling her heart race, preparing for the real confrontation. There he was. Sitting at the bar, chatting idly with the elf Diarmuid Astrid, and lazily swirling a blood-red glass of wine in his hand.

Malavic's conversation died out, and he looked around for the source of the sudden silence in the rowdy pub. Their eyes met. A grin like a glass shard appeared on his lips.

Cocky son of a devil, Bloom thought. One night together, and he just assumed she'd come here just for more? She'd show him. She'd teach him to think he had her figured out.

She marched over as pub goers stepped aside to make way.

In no hurry, Malavic set down his glass and slipped off the barstool and onto his feet. "Gabrielle, I'm so glad you could join—"

She shot the gold binds from her palms in a heartbeat, and they snapped his wrists together in front of him. "You're coming with me, Malavic."

His knowing smirk was gone, replaced by a small O of surprise as he looked from his tied wrists back up to the sheriff's stern face. "And what is it you think I've done?"

"Oh please," she said, wrapping a hand around the back of his neck and steering him ahead of her toward the exit. "Don't act like you have no idea. I know how to do my job." Before they reached the door, she turned back around to the slack-jawed onlookers and said, "Have a good rest of your night, and make sure you and your friends get home safe, everyone."

Then she sent out a wave of Heavenly relief to ease the tension and nudge the witnesses to this arrest to relax and not think twice about what they'd just seen.

"Really, Gabrielle, I would like to know what it is you think I've done. Odds are, you're correct, but I'd still like to be informed."

The door slammed shut behind them as they entered into a warm Eastwind evening.

She didn't answer him, just grabbed him firmly on one bicep and dragged him in step with her down the road.

"Was it something to do with the leprechauns?" Malavic continued. "I promise you, it wasn't blackmail. At least, not really. How *can* it be when I don't actually have anything incriminating on them? They only think I do, ergo the monthly payments. But that hardly counts, and I think we both know you lack the evidence for that to stand up in court."

Still, she said nothing, though Sebastian's arrangement with the leprechauns *was* an interesting lead to follow up on later.

"Not the leprechauns then? Ah, it must be related to the elevated interest rate I instituted with Whirligig. I didn't know you had a nose for financial crime, though. Or is it something— Wait a second." He looked around, blinking. "Jail is the other way. Where are you... Oh." He chuckled.

Was this a mistake? Probably. But even an angel deserved a little diversion every now and then.

The count picked up the pace, coming along willingly now, but she kept a firm grip on him anyway.

"Shall I struggle?" he asked. "Would you like it better if I put up a real fight? Maybe I should run so you *really* have to tie me up."

"Less is more, Sebastian. I'm not here for the conversation."

He chuckled again but said no more as they reached the edge of town and took the path leading back to his castle in the middle of Widow Lake.

Chapter Twenty-Four

Presently

"Gabby? Gabby Bloom. Anybody home?"

The sheriff shook her head to clear it of a memory from long ago that she *definitely* should not have been thinking about just then. She blinked and her eyes focused on the Fifth Wind witch sitting across the table from her in the cozy space of A New Leaf.

"What is it?" Ruby asked. "Oh! Did something click? Do you know what the words on Sophia's wall mean?"

"No, not definitively. I was just thinking of Malavic." She sipped her tea and the liquorish root settled her more firmly in the present.

"Yes," Ruby said, "it *is* curious with him. It seems like he *must* be connected, but how?"

Sheriff Bloom suppressed a mischievous grin. "Stu Manchester found you quickly this morning." It was both a change of subject and not at all a change of subject.

"Yes, well." The Fifth Wind stuffed her mouth with a large chunk of the lemon poppyseed muffin in front of her, presumably to avoid saying more.

Bloom watched her closely over her teacup, getting her kicks where she could. "Did you at least get any useful information out of him?"

"About the case? No, I'm afraid not. But he did show me an interesting room in his home."

The sheriff sighed and nodded. "Let me guess. The library? Where he keeps the things from his old life?"

Ruby paused with the next chunk of her muffin already pinched between her fingers. "Yes, actually. How did you...?"

Bloom chuckled. "He's shown me that as well. A long time ago, don't worry. No hard feelings here. Am I to assume it was as effective a trick on you as it was on me?"

Rather than confirm directly, Ruby tossed the chunk of muffin down onto her plate with a huff. "For fang's sake! The man is *insufferable*."

"He knows how to play on one's sympathy, that's for sure."

"Among other things," Ruby added.

Bloom wouldn't argue with that. Sebastian Malavic had mastered seduction as both a science and an art. Goddess help whoever he set his sights on. "Do you regret it?"

The Fifth Wind's gaze drifted over to her familiar, curled by the fire. "No."

"I'm glad to hear it. We don't need to speak further on the subject then. Back to the case?"

"Sounds good to me. You know, I had a thought."

Ruby leaned forward and so did Bloom. "The writing: *bring it back*. As far as I can see, there are only two 'it's in this case. The first is that stuffed hellhound."

"I had the same thought. Head Healer Ryker said Sophia was attached to it, and she had to take it away to sew it back up."

"Could it be as simple as that, then?" Ruby asked. "Could she have been demanding to have the toy returned to her?"

"Unfortunately," said the sheriff, "no. That doesn't seem to fit. Before you arrived, I asked Ryker when she'd returned the stuffed animal. She got it back to Sophia last night, and there was no writing on the wall at that point."

"Hmm..." Ruby mulled it over as she nibbled at her muffin. "Then the only other 'it' I can think of is the gem. And if Sophia's writing is to be believed, that means that Anastasia has told us another lie. She wasn't in the asylum to deliver the gem, but to take it."

"Head Healer Ryker said she didn't recognize the stone, though. Seems like she would have known if Sophia had something like that with her."

"Not necessarily," Ruby said. "It could have been hidden within the cell. Perhaps in a toy?"

Bloom nodded immediately. "Ryker did say the stuffed hellhound predated her own employment."

"And the toy was found gutted immediately after the murder."

Bloom tore a strip from her warm chocolate croissant and popped it in her mouth as she let the remaining questions rise to the surface of her mind. This was truly the best part of her job, sitting here by a warm fire, sipping tea, and eating something sweet and freshly baked, giving her wings a rest while her mind was allowed to run free. And the fact that she got to enjoy it with Ruby True made the whole experience even better. It was really a shame someone had to die before she could justify the time for such a pleasure. "The matter of Anastasia's movements is still a mystery. How did she get into the asylum, let alone into Sophia's cell and then out again, without setting off alarms or being noticed by the staff? Don't forget, I didn't read any specific guilt or deception on their part when I interviewed them."

"And you're sure you interviewed all of them?"

"Ryker said so. Then there's the matter of the wooden stake. Who just carries a stake with them? Considering we have only one vampire in the realm and he's only predatory in his seduction and lending practices, I don't see that anyone would feel the need to have one on hand. Which means, of course, that someone knew Anastasia would be there and came prepared. Any guesses as to who that might have been?"

Ruby shrugged. "Malavic? If only he didn't have an alibi."

"Is that it?"

"Sophia Gerards certainly has a motive," Ruby conceded, "if our theory about the stolen gem is correct. And she had opportunity, if Anastasia gained entry to her cell briefly, but she still doesn't have the means. For one, she's a waif, and I have a feeling she couldn't muster the strength to plunge a stake through a taut sheet of parchment, let alone another being. But also, where would she have gotten the stake?"

Bloom nodded, leaning back in her chair and allowing herself a moment to think. There had to be a path forward from here, something she'd overlooked.

There always was. She was but one woman, albeit a highly competent and experienced one. Being in charge of the evidence gathering, interviewing suspects, and following up on leads was a lot for a single mind to handle without something falling through the cracks. And while it was nice to have Ruby and her gifts as help, the Fifth Wind was imperfect as well... and clearly preoccupied with other matters. Bloom understood how that could go. There was a limited blood supply in a single person's body, and when it was so busy fueling the palpitations of the heart, there was often little left for the brain, let alone the eyes and ears.

"I think I'd better speak with Sebastian again," Ruby said. "I just *know* he's hiding something."

Sheriff Bloom bit back a grin. "And you think you'll find it in his trousers?"

Ruby gasped and reached across the table and smacked the angel on the arm. "*Really*, Gabby! Give me a little more credit than that." But the Fifth Wind was unable to keep a sneaky grin at bay herself.

"No judgment here, just an observation. I doubt you'll get much out of him at this point. It's easy to fall under his spell."

Ruby sighed. "I suppose you would know."

"I would. That library trick of his is just the start."

"How long did it last for you?" Ruby asked.

Bloom brought her teacup to her lips and paused. "I'm a little embarrassed to admit." She let the fragrant warm drink wash over her tongue.

"Considering this is the second time I've fallen prey, I hardly think you should—"

"Eight years."

"Eight years?!"

Bloom set down her cup with a clatter. "Now! I think if I, an avenging angel, can reserve *my* judgment, you could try at it a little harder. Besides, eight years is a blink of an eye to immortals."

"I apologize, but I'd always assumed your experience was in much the same capacity as mine—once... or now twice. But *years*, well, that's not a series of bad decisions, Gabby, that's a relationship! Were you two *in love?*"

"Far from it. But yes, I did get to know him pretty well over that period of time."

"And you're sure you're not upset with me for encroaching?"

Bloom laughed. "Encroaching on what? I ended it because I had to. The scandal of it would have given every second Eastwinder a simultaneous heart attack out of sheer delight if they'd found out. The High Council would have gone into crisis."

Ruby leaned closer over the table. "How did you manage to keep it a secret?"

Bloom grinned, returning to the same memory she'd been lost in moments earlier. "I arrested him. A lot. It was the only obvious reason he and I would ever be seen together. An angel sheriff and a vampire? Eventually, people did begin to gossip after the arrests became too frequent."

"I can imagine! I'm surprised the *Eastwind Watch* didn't pick up the rumors and run with them!"

"Oh, they did. But they got the story all wrong."

Bloom laughed. "Everyone did. They believed Count Malavic was at the head of some sort of inter-realm crime syndicate."

Ruby cackled. "Oh, I can only imagine the damage that did to his reputation as a philanthropist!"

"Not at all. You'd be surprised what people excuse in a man who gives them money. And he seemed to revel in the challenge to his reputation. Suddenly, he was both the most loved *and* feared man in Eastwind. It was a good run for him. But I knew that it wouldn't last. Lies usually don't. I had one too many close calls and finally decided it was time to end it."

"Was he crushed?"

Bloom shrugged. "Who knows. If he was, he never let on."

"And you?"

"Not crushed, but... lonely again, I suppose. Life can get that way."

"Indeed." The Fifth Wind leaned back and stared down into her teacup.

The loneliness had subsided for the sheriff over the next few decades—it was still there (only companionship can ever soothe loneliness properly, Bloom knew), but she'd rediscovered her many ways of distracting from it through work, meditation, and the occasional good book.

But Ruby True didn't have that much time to lose. Maybe another fifty years? The thought of her friend spending so much of it with that deep, endless yearning for another was almost more than Bloom could stand.

"You know what?" Bloom began. "Maybe you *should* go speak to the count again. No matter *what* happens, you'll get something useful out of him."

Ruby eyed her skeptically. "And you? What will you be doing in the meantime?"

"I thought I'd pop over to the Eastwind Library. I have a farfetched theory forming, but I need to learn a little more about skarbniks first."

Chapter Twenty-Five

101 years before the present...

Sheriff Bloom fastened the top button of her sheriff's uniform while Sebastian Malavic lounged in bed. He'd long since stopped slipping off to his coffin at the end of her visits. While it was nice to have settled into a comfortable routine with someone else, she knew their relationship was teetering dangerously close to just that: a relationship. It couldn't last, but, for now, it was nice.

The count sighed, his baseline of ennui settling in again now that she was preparing to leave. "What if today's the day no owls come screeching out of the clear blue for you, Gabrielle? You waste an entire day in that big, empty station that you could be spending with me instead."

She shot him a quick sideways glance. "If that happens, it would be a first. And I happen to *like* the new building. It's nice and open. And the cells are far enough away from my office that I can't hear the inhabitants calling me all sorts of things that would make a gentler angel blush."

The count reached out and grabbed her, pulling her back onto the bed. She gazed down at him where she sat.

"I'm so glad to hear you like the new building," he said. "I'm still hearing about the cost of it from Liberty. But more importantly, I feel obliged to say just how grateful I am that you are *no gentle angel*."

She rolled her eyes and pushed to her feet again. "There you go, getting sappy on me again, Sebastian."

"Stay for breakfast."

"I can pick up pastries on the way to the station."

"Then stay for coffee. Please."

She slipped on one of her boots but paused to look him over. "Fine. Coffee. Then I *really* need to go to work."

But before she could get her toes into the other boot, there was a loud banging at the front door of the castle, and she whirled around to stare wide-eyed at Sebastian.

"Oh right," he said, grinning mischievously. "I forgot to mention, I've invited the rest of the High Council over for breakfast as well."

If he hadn't already been soulless, the glare she shot him would have made his soul wither. "You scheming devil! You're trying to get me caught. Embarrass me."

He shrugged. "Only if you let yourself be embarrassed by it."

This was typical Sebastian, though. All part of the game they played, the power struggle that had seeped into every fiber of their strange relationship.

She looked around for a quick escape. Out a window,

perhaps? But then they might see her flying overhead. Hiding?

She caught herself. She was the sheriff, for Heaven's sake! She shouldn't be sneaking around like a criminal.

And yet...

"If you expose me, you expose yourself as well," she said. "They'll know why you fought for me so hard with the budget."

He threw the covers off and wandered over to a wardrobe to pick out his clothes for the day. "And? What do you suppose they'll do to the man in charge of the treasury? The one who controls the *dragon* that protects this town's coinage, no less? Kick me off the High Council? Besides, everyone has personal reasons for backing the projects they do. I'm no different."

He had a point. It was only *her* reputation and job on the line if the High Council found her here so early in the morning.

"Tell them you invited me to the meeting, too," she said.

He slipped on a shirt and spared her only a brief glance over his shoulder. "No."

"Sebastian!"

The knocking picked up again, and she heard the High Priestess call for anyone inside.

"How about this," Malavic said. "If you want to get away undetected, I do have a secret passage you can use... if you're not too proud to sneak away from my home like a bootlegger or a common thief."

She weighed her options quickly. "Show me the passage."

He nodded, then went to the window facing out on

the front of the castle, opening it and calling down, "Hold your hides! I've just overslept is all. I'll be down in a second."

He led her down the stairs to the entry hall, and she held her breath as she passed in front of the door leading out to the waiting members of the High Council.

Down a set of narrow winding stairs they went next, and Bloom found herself stepping into Sebastian Malavic's dungeon. In their years of clandestine meetings, he'd never once taken her down here, and she preferred it that way—the less she knew about the things he kept hidden, the easier it was for her conscience to keep this up.

The space made her feel claustrophobic. Angels were meant for open air and blue skies, not dark, dim dungeons like this. It was set up half as a study and half as a wine cellar, and she did her best to ignore the purple cloth that levitated in midair and had a soft glow emanating from beneath, as if it had been thrown over a tall lamp. She had a feeling she knew what lie beneath the cloth, and she had *no* desire to investigate further.

"Here," he said, pausing by a round wooden door in the corner of the room that lay flush against the stony floor. He grabbed the edge and lifted, revealing the opening to a dark hole going down, down, down. "Don't worry," he said, "there's a ladder to help you get to the bottom."

Bloom frowned at the narrow chasm. "Getting to the bottom isn't my biggest concern."

"There's an easy route that will let you out behind Sheehan's Pub. You should emerge entirely out of sight, my shame-filled lover."

"You're sure it's safe down there?"

He hitched an eyebrow skeptically. "You're worried about dying, my dear immortal?"

"Not dying. Being stuck in a cave in for all eternity."

"Ah, yes, that *would* be a disappointment." He tilted his head, inspecting her closely. "You don't believe I would come looking for you if you never turned up?"

"No, I don't. And if it's so safe, how come I always see you *walking* from your castle to Sheehan's and back?"

Malavic shrugged. "Because I find walking much more pleasurable. It keeps the door open for trouble to find me. Or me to find it. Tunnels deprive a man of that. They're better for *sneaking*." He winked and Bloom grunted.

"Fine. Tell me how to get there."

He provided a simple set of directions before adding one last warning: "No matter what your curiosity tells you, don't stray from the instructions or you might end up in the very wrong place at the very worst time."

Though she struggled to think of a worse place to be than Malavic's castle during a worse time than when the entire High Council was waiting on his doorstep, Gabby Bloom agreed and then crawled down into the pitch-black tunnel.

Chapter Twenty-Six

❦

Presently

"Take me to Sophia's cell!" Bloom demanded. The two young healers who had just opened the heavy iron door of Veris Bluffs Asylum stared at the sheriff with wide eyes but didn't move.

"I'm sorry, Sheriff," said one, "I'll have to run this by Head Healer Ryker before—"

"Then do it! I don't need both of you to escort me, just one." Bloom was met with no resistance as she pushed past them and made straight for the waif's cell. The healers hurried after her and one set of footsteps peeled off toward the other half of the facility while another continued to clip-clop after her. She didn't need either of them to show her the way, only to let her inside the customized room.

Bloom pressed her face to the small window in the door to Sophia's cell the moment she reached it. "Fallen Grace," she spat. "Let me in. Now."

The healer, a faun who was likely only a few years on the job if that, shook her head, looking horrified. "I don't have a key, Sheriff."

"Fangs and claws," Bloom cursed again, but there was nothing much to do now but wait and hope the other healer could locate and bring Ryker quickly.

As the faun cowered in the corner of the hall, Bloom summoned up what sympathy she could, forcing out, "It's not your fault. I'm not angry with you."

Head Healer Ryker rounded the corner a moment later. "What is it?" she asked. "What's wrong?"

"I'm afraid one of your patients has escaped."

Ryker's eyes went wide, and the normally composed woman jogged the rest of the way to the door, fumbling to get the key out of her pocket. "What? That's not possible."

"It is, and if you'll hurry and let me inside, I'll show you how."

The door swung open, and as Ryker looked around to verify Bloom's claim of an escape, the angel went straight for the bed, the only place in the room where what she'd just learned about skarbniks at the library might lead her.

With a single hand, she turned the bed on its side, and with the other she grabbed the edge of the rug beneath it and flipped it out of the way. The yawning entrance to the tunnel greeted her, but she felt little gratification in having confirmed her theory. Instead, this finding merely presented a new, more urgent problem. Only if she were lucky would this tunnel lead her to the truth of this puzzling case.

"Skarbniks," Bloom said, addressing the head healer. "You never bothered to read anything about them, did you? And why would you? There had never been a problem with her before, and there are none of her kind in this realm outside of these walls. Besides, she was catatonic, or so we thought. But they're diggers, Beatrice. Tunnelers. Their natural habitat is cave systems, where they guard the natural bounty of the earth—ore and *gems*. It's in their blood. They can't rest when the things they were tasked with protecting go missing."

Head Healer Ryker, though still wide-eyed and on high alert, nodded. "The gem. It was *in here* to begin with, wasn't it?"

Bloom nodded. "I don't believe this tunnel to be a fresh one. The waif might have the energy to crawl through one, but nothing you or I saw indicated she might have the strength to create her own. I believe the vampire Anastasia entered through this tunnel to steal the gem. And then *someone* let her out of the cell. But we can settle that matter later. First, we need to find your escaped patient, and quickly."

Ryker's eyebrows rose toward her slicked-back hair. "You expect me to crawl through that tunnel?"

"No. Definitely not. Entering a mysterious tunnel is the fastest way to get buried alive. I don't suggest anyone go down there."

"Then how do we find her?"

Bloom let her gaze tumble down to the dark hole again. "I think I know where it leads. I'll simply meet her at the end."

Chapter Twenty-Seven

Ruby had every intention of making this trip to Malavic's castle an investigative success. Perhaps it was a matter of ego now, but she didn't want to let herself get sucked in again. Not this time.

She knew he would try something else to derail her. If Bloom's tale was any indication, the vampire had seduction mastered. Her hope was that she might be on the look-out enough this time around to neutralize his skills.

And, also, she had Clifford with her now.

She knocked on the thick front doors of the castle and waited. It was nearly lunchtime, and the lemon poppy seed muffin she'd eaten was wearing thin. Her stomach growled.

"Didn't you just eat?" Clifford asked.

"Yes, but it was just a muffin."

"And I suppose you also expended an unusual amount of energy last night."

"Bad dog," she said.

Clifford wagged his tail lazily.

When the door opened, Count Malavic stood at the entrance, grinning. "Speak of the devil!"

"You're one to talk."

"No, it's just that I was about to send for you. I've prepared a surprise. I think you'll like it."

Ruby exchanged a look with Clifford before the hellhound began sniffing the air wafting out from inside.

"Don't you try any tricks with me, Malavic. I just spoke with Sheriff Bloom, and I'm onto you."

"I'd like it if you were, yes."

She scowled. "But I do have questions for you regarding the—" The smell Clifford had already picked up on finally hit her, and she gasped and stared wide-eyed at Malavic. "That's not..."

"Yes." Pleasure dripped from that single word, and he stepped aside and motioned for his visitors to enter.

"It's a trap," Clifford warned as the count closed the door behind them.

"I know it is. But it's a nice one."

Malavic wound an arm around Ruby's waist and led her through the entry hall and into the dining room, where her sense of sight confirmed her sense of smell.

Upon the end of the long table closest to them was a giant platter stacked a foot high with beignets. "Sebastian," she breathed, inhaling the warm, long-lost scent she adored so much.

Beside the platter was a saucer of chocolate sauce and a small bowl, steam issuing from its surface.

Ruby gasped. "Is that...?"

"*Café au lait.* Yes."

She turned to him, staring up into his hungry eyes. "But how did you even know what all this *was*? They don't have this in Eastwind! I don't understand how you managed it."

"It's a mystery you don't need to solve, my dear witch. Just enjoy it. And the longer you wait to do so, the colder it all becomes. It would be a shame not to enjoy the beignets while they're so soft and the chocolate and coffee so hot."

He reached past her and took one of the puffy pastries off the top of the pile, dipping it in the sauce and bringing it to her mouth. She parted her lips slowly, feeling lost, off balance, but at peace with it all. The taste was exactly how she remembered it from the last time she'd visited New Orleans. How he'd managed to match the recipe so exactly when he wasn't himself a baker was a mystery indeed. And the notion that it was one she never had to solve held an appeal all its own.

She finished the bite he'd ripped off for her and noticed a smear of the chocolate sauce that had managed to stay on his fingers. She licked it off... slowly.

"*Ruby,*" came Clifford's warning tone.

"*I'm not as strong or as smart as I thought, Cliff. You're welcome to leave me here.*"

"*It's not that.*"

"*Then what is it?*"

"*We have a visitor.*"

Ruby blinked and licked the remaining powdered sugar off her lips as she regained her balance and looked around.

The thin ghost of Anastasia Vorporal was staring at her from the corner of the dining room. "There's something you need to see," she said.

Ruby tugged free of Malavic's arms, her lusty thoughts turning to instantly to raw agitation. "What is it, then?" she asked the spirit, ignoring the count's confused expression.

"Before you let your guard down around him, there's something you need to see upstairs. I wasn't sure if I would ever find it, but I finally have."

"And why should I believe a word you say?" Ruby demanded. "You told me he murdered you and we've already established that's impossible. You lied to me."

Malavic cut in. "Are you speaking to a ghost? Is that Anastasia from the asylum? Where is she? I'll give that liar a good swatting. Banish her myself for trying to get me locked up. How *dull* that would have been!"

"Hush, Sebastian!" Ruby turned back to the spirit. "Fine. Show me what it is, and perhaps I'll listen to what you have to say."

Anastasia nodded then flickered. "You'll want him to stay down here."

"I'm not afraid of him," Ruby spat. "If he'd wanted to harm me, he could have last night. Lead the way."

Malavic trailed behind the Fifth Wind as she followed the spirit upstairs, but not without Clifford providing a protective buffer between her and the vampire. The hellhound, apparently, wasn't as confident of his witch's safety.

Ruby wasn't much surprised when Anastasia led her directly to the library she'd visited the night before. "I've already seen all this," Ruby said, "and I hardly see how it's relevant to the investigation."

"Just wait. It'll all become clear in a moment."

From the rear, Malavic said, "This isn't nearly as interesting as I'd hoped. Are you sure you want to let your beignets and *café au lait* get cold over this wild weregoose chase?"

Ruby didn't answer because Anastasia had just pulled up short by one of the display cases. "It's fallen under there," she said, pointing to the small, dark space between the display's short wooden legs.

"What is it?" Ruby demanded. Getting on her hands and knees to grope around beneath the piece of furniture was quite a vulnerable position to get into without knowing first what she was even looking for. And to do it on the word of a known liar was even less appealing.

"The other half of that torn charcoal sketch he keeps." Anastasia finished with a smug expression, for it must have been clear as day how much *that* piqued Ruby's interest.

"Fine." She got onto her hands and knees and reached beneath the cabinet. At first, she felt nothing but a continuation of the wood floors.

"Looking for cobwebs?" Malavic asked. "If so, I'm afraid you'll be disappointed. Spiders don't much like cohabitating with vampires, and I do keep this place clean."

Then she felt it, the very edge of the paper. She grunted, stretching the final inch to slide it back to her.

With an effort, she got to her feet and shielded her find away from Malavic's immediate view. Only then did she look properly at what she'd found.

It was blank.

Oh wait.

She flipped it over and when she saw *who* was staring back up at her from the sketch, she gasped and nearly dropped the crucial evidence...

Chapter Twenty-Eight

The smiling face of Sophia Gerards was unmistakable as it stared lovingly toward the rough edge of the sketched portrait. The waif? That was Sebastian's long-lost love? But how?

"You need to run," Anastasia said. "Once he knows what you have, he'll do the same thing to you that he did to her."

But Ruby didn't understand exactly what that meant. What had Sebastian done to this woman? Had he *made* her a waif?

Malavic leaned to look over Ruby's shoulder. "Whatever did you manage to find under—"

Ruby could practically feel the temperature of the room change as the count's words froze in his throat.

"Go!" Anastasia urged. "Run!"

It wasn't a bad suggestion, Ruby thought, as she turned to meet Malavic's murderous eyes. She'd exposed something about him that he'd kept hidden. And for how long?

Ruby's mouth went dry. "Did you do it to her, Sebastian? Are you the reason she's a waif?"

A muscle in his jaw twitched, and the candlelight caught on one of his glistening fangs as his lips pulled back in a sneer. "Yes. I did that to her."

"Run!" urged the spirit again. "Have the hound hold him off, and I'll show you where you can go that's safe from him!"

Clifford, at least, didn't need to be told twice. His lunge at the count was precipitated only a split second by a deep growl. Malavic stumbled back, and it was all Ruby needed.

She wasn't fast by any means, but she had adrenaline on her side. The count blocked her way back out into the hall, but Anastasia wasn't heading in that direction. Instead, she led Ruby to a full-length mirror on the wall. "Pull that," the spirit instructed, pointing at one of the sconces upon which a candle remained unlit.

Ruby grabbed the sconce and yanked, and the mirror became a door, swinging open to reveal nothing but darkness behind it.

"*Clifford, come!*"

"*No, you go. I'll be fine.*"

Ruby knew just enough about vampire fighting skills to remain planted in place.

"*He'll kill you!*"

"*No, he won't. He likes me too much. And if he does manage it, I'll just come back as a grim. Now run!*"

The dim figure of Anastasia motioned her forward into the darkness, and Ruby, already hating herself for it, left her familiar behind and stepped through the doorway.

And nearly fell on her face immediately.

"Watch your step. This staircase is old, and the rocks are worn and slick."

"Now you tell me," she grumbled.

Down, down, down, they went, until Ruby was sure she was half a mile underground.

The sound of Clifford's snarls had long since faded, and now there was nothing but her own panting to cut through the grave-like silence.

"This way." The spirit flickered, and a jolt of fear rushed through Ruby's veins. What if Anastasia left her now? Alone in this darkness?

And where exactly were they headed? Perhaps the library. Maybe this tunnel intersected somewhere with the library's underground rooms. Or perhaps she'd come out in the Parchment Catacombs, though she didn't like that thought nearly as much. It was common knowledge that *those* tunnels were long and winding enough that people could get lost in them and never find their way out.

"Just a little further," Anastasia said. Ruby's legs ached from the sudden sprint followed by nearly ten minutes of hurrying after the ghost. Was Clifford okay? She suspected she would have felt it if he were not, but she couldn't be sure. Maybe he and Malavic had worked out their differences? Or perhaps her familiar had made it out the front door of the castle. Could he manage the door handle with his paws?

They took another turn, and then the worst finally happened.

The spirit of Anastasia Vorporal flickered once again and then blinked out entirely.

Ruby was totally alone in the dark.

Chapter Twenty-Nine

Sheriff Bloom already had small icicles forming on the tips of her wings from the long, cold flight before she ever saw Rainbow Falls appear ahead of her. All the pieces of this puzzle were converging in her mind, though precisely what picture they would form in the end was still unclear to her. All she knew was that Sophia was a skarbnik, and one who was fixated on getting the heart-shaped gem back in her possession.

The waterfall was enchanted, though in exactly what way was for the first East Wind witches who founded this town to know and for Gabby Bloom to find out in a few more seconds. She was far more concerned with the obstacle of the water, though, the pounding force of it in its plummeting descent, and whether she could make it all the way through without being crushed down onto the rocks below.

If she had a chance, she needed to pick up speed.

And so she did, beating her wings harder, harder, then at the last second folding them in, folding her arms into her as well, to take the form of an arrow shot from a bow.

As much as she wanted to shut her eyes and brace for impact, she kept them open. Then she pressed her palms together like a diver at the very last moment, and through the falls she went.

The water felt like a hammer to every inch of her body at once, then a split second later, she crashed into something—not solid, but not exactly a downy cloud, either. Her ears rang as she took stock of herself. No strange enchantments to speak of, at least none she could see. No hair sprouting from unusual places or extra digits.

She shook her wings to bead off the water only to realize that they were bone dry, lacking even the small icicles that had accumulated from the flight.

Bloom would have liked to spend a little more time checking herself for ill effects, since most enchantments weren't immediately visible, but there wasn't any time. Not when she was now inside the Eastwind Treasury, where both an obsessive skarbnik waif and a dragon awaited her somewhere.

What had broken her fall was a pile of gold coins, and she quickly untucked the front of her uniform shirt to let a few that had made their way down her collar tumble free and rejoin the others in the pile. And then, of course, she tucked her shirt back in. Presentation mattered.

But where to go now? The light that made it through the falls danced and mingled with the soft glow of hovering orbs. Bloom paused; listened. She didn't have to listen long before she heard the sound she was looking for and followed it.

It was two caverns over where the sheriff found

Sophia. The waif was riffling frantically through a mishmash pile of coins and gems.

"Sophia," Bloom called. "Sophia Gerards."

The girl looked up... and growled. "Where is it?" Her voice was raspy, but whether it was normally like that or a result of years without use, Bloom couldn't tell. Either way, the search seemed to have invigorated the waif who had seemed completely catatonic only earlier that day.

"I don't know where it is," Bloom replied. "But I know who would. Count Sebastian Malavic."

Sophia paused from her digging and looked up. And when she did, the walls around them shook.

A small stalactite crashed to the ground just beside Bloom's left boot.

The angel steadied herself. "Do you know him?" she asked. "Does that name mean something to you?"

"Where is it?" Sophia demanded, and when the earth shook again, Bloom knew it could be no coincidence. The skarbnik was making it happen.

"Fangs and claws!" came a familiar voice. Gabby Bloom turned to find Ruby True practically spilling out of a dark passage on the far side of the very same cavern. The Fifth Wind witch looked around. "Oh, thank goddess! I'm somewhere! Wait. Oh no. I'm *here*?" Then she looked around and realized she had company. "Gabby!" She took a few hurried steps toward the angel before Bloom shot out her hand and motioned for her to stop. Ruby pulled up short.

"Don't startle her," Bloom whispered just enough for her voice to carry through the large but quiet space. She nodded toward Sophia, and Ruby's eyes went large.

"It's *her*," the Fifth Wind witch breathed. Ruby crept

over as the sheriff returned her cautious attention to the manic waif.

Sophia poked her head up like she'd just caught a scent, then shuffled on to the next cavern down. Ruby and Bloom inched quietly after her.

"What's the plan?" Ruby whispered.

"Plan?" Bloom said. "I was just trying to apprehend Sophia to keep her safe, but it seems we have a new problem on our hands."

"And that is?"

"She can cause earthquakes."

"Ah, swirls," Ruby cursed. "I was hoping your problem would be the same as my problem, but it isn't. So now we have two problems."

"Oh, I suspect we have many more than that, but what's the one you brought?"

Ahead of them, Sophia had paused and was scanning the wide room with a dazed expression.

"That," Ruby said, pointing at the waif, "is Malavic's long-lost love."

"*What?*" Bloom hissed. She looked back at the girl who appeared to be no older than twenty. Of course, she had many more years than that, just ageless ones. "Are you sure?"

Ruby pulled out the torn sketch. "Yes, fairly."

Sheriff Bloom couldn't believe what she was looking at, but it made sense, and she knew right away what was on the missing half of that page. Malavic had shown it to her over a century ago, but it seemed like only yesterday. The recollections still smelled like fresh-turned earth.

More of the pieces began to click into place now, and

Bloom was starting to see a full image come together when Sophia cackled.

The waif had found it, and stood atop the pile of similar stones, holding the one from the pedestal up to examine it.

"Sophia, dear," Ruby said, moving forward. "You need to come with us."

Another tremor beneath their feet, a frightful glare from the waif, and Ruby stopped in her tracks.

"Don't move," came yet another voice, and Bloom turned to find Malavic striding purposefully toward them.

Bloom was caught off guard as Ruby dived behind her and demanded, "What have you done with Clifford?"

Malavic paused in his progress to glare at her. "You're worried about *Clifford?* Oh, he's just fine. But do you ask how *I* am after a fierce, and dare I say *uncalled for* hellhound savaging? I'll be pulling his fur out of my mouth for years to come!" Malavic turned toward the waif. "Sophia. Bring it to me."

The waif looked up, eyes glassy and vacant, and when she spotted the count, a glimmer of recognition colored her ashen complexion.

"Sophia, my love." The count inched closer. "It's okay. You've had a scare, but things will be okay now."

The earth shook fiercely then, causing Malavic to pull up short.

"Why's she doing that?" Ruby asked.

He didn't spare her a glance as he replied, "To bring the ceiling down upon us, obviously. To collapse the earth and bury us all alive."

"Oh."

Bloom whispered, "Skarbniks are burrowing people."

"Is that supposed to comfort me, Gabby?" Ruby hissed.

"Sophia," Malavic continued, risking another step closer while the girl continued to clutch the gem to her chest. "It's me. Sebastian. You know I won't... You're safe. You can keep the Pulse Stone."

"You took it," the waif rasped.

"No. I didn't. Someone else did. But I should have brought it back to you rather than keeping it here. That was my mistake."

"You wanted it for yourself. You wanted to take it from me."

"No, my love. I've taken enough. I don't want a single thing more from you. All I want now is to give. Please. Don't be afraid."

Sophia took a tentative step closer to him and paused, but that was all the invitation he needed. Malavic rushed forward and pulled the waif into his arms, and she let him. No more earthquakes, just a deep, mournful silence as the other women looked on.

Still cradling Sophia in his arms, he cast a glance to the others. "I need to take her back to Veris Bluffs."

"Not yet," Bloom said. "I think you owe us an explanation."

"Please," he begged, and the tone was unlike Bloom had ever heard from him. "She's exerted herself enough already. She needs to rest."

But Bloom wouldn't be deterred. "She can't die, so she can wait. You're not going anywhere until you tell me what's going on. How do you know Anastasia Vorporal? Did you kill her?"

"I didn't kill her," he said. "I couldn't if I tried. She's the one vampire I couldn't touch."

Through the orange glow of the cavern, Bloom narrowed her eyes at the count. "And why is that?"

"Because," he said, "Anastasia is the one who made me."

Chapter Thirty

❧❦❧

"She's your sire?" Sheriff Bloom gaped, and Ruby could hardly believe it either, yet it was all starting to make a strange sort of sense.

"She is," said Malavic, still hugging the weak girl to his chest.

"But wait," Ruby said, "you told me vampires can sense their sires. That means you would have known when she entered the realm."

"And I did."

"You lied."

He scoffed. "Of course."

"So, you sensed she had entered, and you killed her," Ruby said.

Malavic sighed. "How many times... No, *I* didn't kill her. I was with Ted and then you and then Ted again, as you both should know."

Bloom said, "But you know who did kill her."

And now a small smirk turned his lips. "I have a pretty good idea."

"Just come out with it, Sebastian," Bloom snapped. "I'm not letting you take Sophia back to Veris Bluff until you do. How long she has to wait is up to you."

He cast his gaze down to the waif in his arms, who seemed in no hurry herself. Instead, she merely cooed over the Pulse Stone in her clutches.

"Before I was a vampire, I was a skarbnik. Sophia was my love. Together, we guarded the caves of Veriarch in the realm of Sangorn. Every cavern has its own Pulse Stone. People think of underground as a still, dead place, but it's the opposite. There's an entire living, thriving world in places like this, and the Pulse Stone keeps all of it healthy and vibrant, keeps the earth producing gems, keeps the water flowing smoothly. They are incredibly valuable, Pulse Stones. All kinds of powerful potions can be made from them, which is why they must be guarded." He paused. "Anastasia stole ours, and I was forced to hunt her down. But it was a trap. A lure. I was able to track the stone to her home, where I spied it through her front window. I should have known. I should have sensed that something was amiss, but I was too focused on getting back what was mine. Skarbniks can have a one-track mind about that sort of thing." He nodded down to the girl in his arms. "Anastasia set upon me, turned me. And all before I ever found the gem. I fled, naturally, to complete the painful transformation, but I knew that so long as Anastasia still had it, Sophia would want it back, and she, too, might fall prey to the same trap.

"I wanted to stay away, far away, once I became *this*, but I had no choice but to make one last trek into town. My plan was to steal back the gem, return it to the cave, and disappear forever. But it didn't work out that way.

With my newfound strength and stealth, I did manage to secure the gem from my cursed sire, but I was caught in the act of returning it. Sophia interrupted that step of the process.

"All my feelings for her came flooding back to me in a rush, only this time they were filtered through the bloodlust of my new condition. I wanted her to be mine forever, like I always had, only now it took on a different hue. I wanted her in a new way, not as a man desires a companion, but as a conqueror desires a claim.

"I was still new to vampirism, inexperienced, unable to control my urges, and I set upon her before I could stop myself, draining her near to death. But before I could complete the ritual, she said a single word that stopped me." He paused. "She said my name. I'd almost lost myself, but she brought me back. Too late for her, though. I knew the harm was already upon her, but I also knew I couldn't complete the transformation. I couldn't thrust upon her the same bloodlust, the same *damnation* that I now faced for eternity.

"And so I fled. I took Sophia and the Pulse Stone, knowing it would become little more than a rock once we had left Sangorn. I packed all the things from our world that I could carry in my luggage, and I stole away to find a new world for us, somewhere I could be the only vampire, so as not to learn the loathsome ways of my kind, and where she could be safe, anonymous, but taken care of and united with the only thing she remained attached to: the Pulse Stone of our old life."

The count seemed to lose himself in reverie, and Bloom took the opportunity to speak. "You built it, didn't you? You financed and led the effort for Veris Bluffs

Asylum ages ago. I remember it being built, but I didn't pay attention to how or why."

"I did. Under one condition: a special room be made up for her, and her connection to me be erased from the ledgers. Hundreds of years it's been. But finally the truth has been unearthed."

Something fell into place suddenly in Ruby's mind. "And when Anastasia broke into Sophia's cell, you must have sensed it, too. Sofia may not be a full vampire, but am I correct in assuming that the half-life you've given her as a waif still connects the two of you, as if you were her sire?"

Malavic nodded. "Her blood runs through me. I felt when Anastasia had arrived, but I was confident she wouldn't be able to trace the Pulse Stone. However, when I felt Sophia's distress, I knew I'd been too sure of myself. I sent an emergency owl over to the Asylum, and after that, I'm not sure what happened, only that Anastasia was dead, and Sophia was safe. Nothing else mattered to me."

"He's lying!" came another voice, the source of which appeared beside Sophia and Malavic.

Ruby rolled her eyes. "Not you again."

The shade of Anastasia Vorporal said, "Huh?"

"I can't trust a word you say," Ruby explained, while the other three living beings, unable to see what she was, merely looked on. "But I think I understand how you're here." She turned to the count. "You said Sophia's blood runs through your veins. Am I to take it that the ritual of creating a new vampire also requires the sire to give the victim some of her blood?"

"Yes, but I never gave Sophia any—"

"I'm not talking about Sophia. I'm talking about you. Some of Anastasia's blood runs through your veins."

He nodded, and Ruby turned to Bloom, whose sharp eyes showed dawning comprehension.

Ruby turned back to Anastasia. "Normally, when a spirit comes to see me, it's because they have unfinished business. They won't rest until their murderer is apprehended, that sort of thing."

"So?" Anastasia demanded. "Why haven't you apprehended my murder and set me free? He's right there!"

"Give it a rest," Ruby said. "We know it couldn't have been him. I believe I know who it was, but that's beside the point. Because I don't think that arresting the guilty party will send you off into the afterlife." The cave was deathly silent as Ruby gathered her final thoughts and went on. "I've been curious from the start about two things: how a vampire's spirit could appear, and why yours is so thin. You're clearly not a typical ghost, and I would know since I see quite a few of them but never one like you. As I said, the others have one thing in common: unfinished business. It tethers them to the mortal plane, to their flesh... and blood. The unfinished business, the need for revenge that is tethering you to this plane is not your own. Instead, I believe it runs through Sebastian's veins. It's the hatred for all you've taken from him, the sense of injustice that he can never make you suffer the way he has, because of your actions. So long as that need for vengeance boils within his blood—and your blood— you will be tethered here in your own hopeless half-life. You won't be able to move on of your own accord."

The spirit was glowing brighter than ever now, and

Ruby could sense the desperation in it. She went on: "Why did you travel all this way to steal back the Pulse Stone? Were you a skarbnik before? No, I think not. I don't believe it was ever about the Pulse Stone at all, but rather what you thought the stone might bring with it. Your progeny. Malavic. You thought that if you stole the gem, he would be forced to follow you. As long as you controlled it, you controlled him. It was loneliness, then, wasn't it? After so many years of being a monster, were you craving a companion without the slightest clue how to find one? Is that why you turned him those centuries ago? Misery loves company. The victim becomes the victimizer. You must have been in a dark place."

"You don't know anything about me!" Anastasia raged, glowing brighter.

"Sebastian ended it. He nearly continued the vicious cycle with Sophia, but unlike you, he was able to stop himself at the last second. He harmed her, yes, but then he tried to make it right. And he managed not to hurt her so badly that she would harm others. She's no killer, and we all have Sebastian to thank for that." Ruby felt her own loathing for this spirit growing as she continued to spin the tale and saw plainly on Anastasia's face that she was striking gold with each new accusation.

"I had no choice," Anastasia growled. "You don't know what it's like! You can't control the hunger."

"And yet Sebastian did. And he still does... to some extent." Ruby shot him a sideways glance. "Don't fool yourself, Anastasia. You had a choice then, and you have one now... If your release from this plane hinged *entirely* upon the count's forgiveness, I would tell you to plan on lingering in this state for eternity. But there is one other option. I can banish you."

"Ruby," Bloom said quietly.

But Ruby held firm, her spine like an iron rod. She didn't relish the prospect either. Banishment was to give up, to push through the natural order things, to admit that there was no healing, no growth, no change possible. Spirits remained tethered to the physical plane in order to heal some wound before moving on and being reborn, fresh. What happened when that process was skipped? Ruby didn't wish to think on it now.

Because in the end, Anastasia had had centuries to do the right thing, to change her patterns to something less harmful to others, and she hadn't. That wasn't Ruby's burden to carry.

"Banish me?" Anastasia said, almost laughing. "You think *you* can banish *me*?"

"I do."

"I'd like to see you try."

"Very well," Ruby said. And then the Fifth Wind closed her eyes and slipped to the In-Between, psychically dragging Anastasia there with her.

The vampire blinked in the bright light of the park by the pond, and gasped when she looked down to see her body not as a wisp, but in full flesh.

Ruby took her in and felt a pang of regret for what she intended to do. Who was she to say when anyone was past the point of no return? Who was she to decide that Anastasia had no hope of changing course, of seeing the error of her predatory and self-serving ways, of learning to stop feeding that black hole inside her so that it might blink out and make room for the light to shine through again?

But before the doubt could take root, the vampire, finding herself back in her flesh, bared her fangs. Her first words to Ruby said all there was left to say. "I can feed again!"

Anger rose up inside the Fifth Wind at this shade who threatened to taint this special In-Between world with her unharnessed bloodlust. Ruby's protective instincts took over from there.

A thought was all it took, a silent desire, and then the witch felt her fingers tighten around a wooden stake. She didn't hesitate now, just drove her weapon straight into the vampire's chest.

The end came swiftly, as Anastasia collapsed in on herself, and Ruby felt her remaining energy sucked from her body and into the vortex where the vampire had just stood. She stumbled forward and fell face first into the soft green grass, feeling as if the wind had just been knocked out of her. She mustered what few drops of strength remained to roll over onto her side. The spirits passing by on the footpath by the lake hardly seemed to notice the massive disturbance. They were souls of pain, after all, and while suffering often attracted more suffering, it could also numb one to the suffering of others.

But not Ruby. She felt the pain of Anastasia Vorporal acutely now. Because while both vampire and psychic were alone among the worlds, Ruby, at least, still stood a chance of someday finding what her soul most needed. And that knowledge was enough to make her mourn for the shade damaged beyond repair, even as she knew it was her job to rid the realm of such a dark force. Now spent and sure it was over, Ruby fell back onto the grass.

She opened her eyes and found herself again in the treasury. She was on her back staring up at the stalactites above. She must have fallen, except she was certain that would have hurt, yet nothing in her body throbbed...

She rocked her head to the side and realize she wasn't on the floor at all. She was cradled in Bloom's arms. The angel must have caught her before she could hit the hard ground.

The Sheriff addressed Malavic. "Go. Get Sophia back to Veris Bluffs. And then wait for me. I believe you and Head Healer Ryker owe me a more detailed explanation."

Sebastian nodded and guided Sophia away, or at least that was what it looked like to Ruby through her blurry vision.

Her head swam. She gazed up into Bloom's face as the angel carried her easily. "My hero," Ruby muttered.

Gabby Bloom grunted. "You're delusional. Probably best if you don't speak for a while. Hold on as best you can, though. Getting back out through that waterfall is going to be a trick..."

Chapter Thirty-One

Ruby awoke in her reading chair, which was convenient, considering she had just dreamed of a tortured but handsome werewolf duke, and the book on the table next to her chair was the third book of the *Royal Canine* series she had yet to finish. *The Werewolf Heir's Sordid Affair* wouldn't read itself…

The only concerning thing about her current predicament was that she didn't remember getting into this chair in the first place. She also didn't remember putting the blanket over her lap or changing into her warmest pajamas or grabbing her slippers from her bedroom or stoking the fire in the hearth.

She yawned loudly and Clifford raised his head from where he lounged on the rug by the fireplace. *"You're up finally."*

"How long did I sleep?"

"Only a handful of hours. I wasn't sure if I should wake you or let you sleep through the whole night."

She rocked her head from side to side, stretching her

stiff neck. "I must have been in some state when I got home. I don't even remember the walk."

"Because you didn't walk. Gabby flew you back."

And now the memories came to her in a rush, and she felt tired all over again. "And did she also help me into my pj's?"

Clifford wagged his tail in the affirmative.

"For fang's sake," she muttered. "As if the sheriff doesn't have anything better to do than babysit *my* hide." And then another memory came crashing back into her skull. "Cliff! Are you all right?" Against the clicks and clacks of her protesting ankles and knees, she stood quickly and rushed over to him, settling next to him on the floor and running her hand over his soft red fur.

"I'm fine. The count hardly fought back."

"Oh, Cliff." She hugged him tightly around the neck. "It's a good thing you're so lovable."

His tail slapped against the rug in a string of dull thumps. *"We played fair. But to be honest, I think he didn't want to hurt me because he was afraid it would hurt you."*

"Don't be silly. He doesn't care either way about me."

The next half hour was spent filling in her familiar on the events in the treasury while she made herself a pot of lavender and mint tea.

She was just about to pour her second cup when there was a rapping at her front door. She knew immediately who it must be.

Grinning, she went to answer the door.

Gabby Bloom inhaled deeply. "I hope you can spare me a cup of whatever you're brewing."

A light snow had begun to fall, glittering in the

moonlight on its gentle way down to the earth. "Of course. Come on in."

Bloom took off her boots at the door and hung up her coat before stepping further inside. "Just came from Veris Bluffs."

"Not the station? I assumed you would have made an arrest."

The angel's large wings hung down on either side of the chair as she settled in at Ruby's old wooden parlor table. "No one to arrest."

"But it *was* Head Healer Ryker who murdered the vampire, wasn't it?"

"So you figured that out, eh?"

"Only through process of elimination, and after talking it through with Clifford. It wasn't Sebastian, I think it's obvious that it wasn't Sophia, and you interviewed each of the healers working when the body was found. Except for Ryker."

Ruby brought over a fresh kettle and another mug.

"Ah, yes," Bloom said, "I even *knew* there was something I was overlooking. Head Healer Ryker seems so obvious in retrospect."

"You weren't the only one who missed it," Ruby said, filling both cups before taking a seat across from the sheriff. "The thought never even crossed my mind until this evening. She was the one who sent you the emergency owl, for fang's sake."

"She admitted to it right away, once I confronted her in her office. It seemed her reluctance sprang not from self-preservation, but some sort of *deal* with Count Malavic. Once he gave her the go-ahead, she was happy to comply."

"Of *course* she had a deal with him." Ruby rolled her eyes. "It seems like everyone in town does. How did it happen, then?"

Bloom inhaled the lavender and mint steam before explaining. "Malavic sensed Sophia's disturbance while at Sheehan's Pub with Ted and sent urgent word to Ryker via owl. Ryker then hurried to Sophia's cell and found the waif fighting off Anastasia, who was trying to get back to the tunnel she'd crept in from."

"I didn't think Sophia had it in her to fight a vampire," Ruby said. "But then again, if it was to defend the Pulse Stone, maybe so. She was certainly invigorated down in the treasury while she searched for it. And what about that tunnel? That was there long before the murder, wasn't it?"

"Yes," said Bloom. "Malavic confirmed that for me. Apparently, back when the asylum was being built, he made sure it was included in the blueprints. I assume he paid off anyone who knew about it generously enough to keep it secret until those with the knowledge passed away. He wanted to leave the option open of visiting her without anyone knowing."

"Sophia could have escaped, though."

"Yes, but why? The Pulse Stone was already there with her, buried in the hellhound. She had no desire to be anywhere else. All she cared about was right there in that cell with her."

"True. So, Anastasia found her through the tunnel that connects the treasury to the asylum. She sustained the burn from Maggie the dragon while she was down there, then emerged in Sophia's cell after who-knows-how-much wandering. Seems a lucky break."

Bloom conceded with a nod. "It does. But not as lucky as you think. According to the count, anyone who touches a Pulse Stone while it's full of magic has the ability to track it. That's how he found it when Anastasia stole it originally."

"Ah," Ruby said. "But you or I couldn't track it because it was already dead when we handled it. I see. Then it makes sense that Anastasia might have followed the pull of it to Veris Bluffs and realized there was little chance of her walking in through the front door. She then concluded that there was a very good chance that, with two former skarbniks involved, there would be a tunnel system she could exploit."

"Exactly," said Bloom. "She must have done a little sleuthing herself, and when she learned Malavic was the town treasurer and had sole access to the cave, the idea of where some of the tunnels might connect became clear to her."

"She must not have heard about the dragon, though. Or else she was willing to risk it." Ruby paused, letting her thoughts organize further. "Ryker intervened in the fight between Sophia and the vampire, then? She would have had enough notice about the specifics of the danger to grab a stake before entering the cell."

"In short, yes. Then she dragged the body out into the other side of the asylum to avoid any connection back to Sophia."

Ruby sipped her tea, letting the final pieces fall into place. "And it would have worked, wouldn't it? It would have remained a mystery were it not for that one unexpected hitch: Anastasia's restless spirit."

"Indeed." Bloom sipped her tea and moaned, her

shoulders visibly relaxing. "While I'm usually one for coffee over tea, this is delicious. Anyway, no one could have foreseen that Anastasia would stick around in spirit form. And if it weren't for her pointing us back to Sophia's room, our investigation might have immediately hit a dead end."

"No pun intended, I'm sure."

Bloom inspected her closely over her teacup. "How are you doing?"

"Oh, you know. Tired, unsettled."

"I imagine. Banishing is no small feat."

"Was I wrong to do it?" Ruby held her breath, but she wasn't forced to wait long for the reply.

"No," Bloom said firmly. "I don't believe you were. Like you said, there was no perfect option, but that wasn't your making. It was a result of Anastasia's actions over a span of hundreds, perhaps thousands of years. I know it's unpleasant to think that some people who might have started off good have passed the point of redemption. But it was always their *choice*. Look at Sebastian. He's insufferable, yes. Scheming, sure. But he made the choice to come to Eastwind and live as normal of a life as he could, given his circumstances. And it's not like he hasn't done anything good for anyone. Sure, he uses his financial contributions as leverage, but he's also done a good job of keeping the town safe from other vampires. He doesn't want the people of this town to suffer the way he has."

"You almost make him out to sound like a gentleman."

Bloom scoffed. "I think you and I *both* know that's not the case."

Ruby chuckled. "Not even a little bit." A pleasant silence passed between them before Ruby spoke again. "I think I'm done with him. I mean, let's be honest, he's not exactly my type."

The angel eyed her skeptically. "For good this time?"

"At least until the next heartbreak."

Bloom raised her mug. "Then here's to no more heartbreak."

"I'll drink to that." She raised her tea as well, and the women drank to it.

Ruby's gaze drifted to the roaring fire, the one Bloom had stoked before leaving to wrap up the case. She sighed. "It's hard to make sound decisions when you're lonely."

"Almost impossible," agreed the sheriff.

Ruby returned her attention to her guest across the table. "Yet, I'm feeling of sounder mind by the second, now that you're here, old friend."

The postal bell rang outside, and the women exchanged a puzzled look before Ruby went to check. Who could be sending her a letter this late at night?

She opened the front door, hugging herself against the winter chill. A pygmy owl was resting after having dropped the message into the box below, its wings pulled in tight, head tucked close to its body. She would have invited it inside, but she knew it would never come. Mail owls took their job seriously. Their professionalism never flagged. Accepting that small kindness might create an indebtedness that owls would never tolerate.

She pulled the message from the drop box and stepped back inside, shutting out the snowy night before unrolling the parchment and reading it over silently.

Ruby,

I can't stop thinking about you. I don't know how it could work between us, but I need to see you tonight. Please. Filaemenia was only a distraction. What you and I had was something different. If you still want me like I want you, send your reply and I'll be at your doorstep within the hour.

-Z

"Who in Heaven's name is sending you letters at this time of night?" Bloom asked, though her tone indicated she was less concerned with the possible impropriety and more interested in the juicy gossip the letter might bring.

Ruby read it over again, her heart fluttering wildly. It certainly was nice to be wanted like this, and by a werebear as handsome and confident as Zax Banderfield, no less. He was practically begging her to invite him over at this late hour. She knew what that meant. It could be quite fun...

After a moment's more consideration, she crossed the room and tossed the letter into the fire. "Just a letter from a poor decision waiting to be made. But like I said, I'm feeling sounder by the minute. Now, where were we? Oh yes, you were going to tell me about the eight years you spent courting Sebastian."

Bloom laughed. "Was I?"

Ruby settled herself at the parlor table again. "Yes, you were. And I was going to pour you another cup of hot tea while you did."

"Ah," Bloom said, nodding, "but if you want to hear *those* kinds of stories, we're both going to need something a little stronger than tea."

Ruby grinned. "What kind of friend would I be if I didn't keep something stronger on hand for a time such as this? I think I have a bottle of whiskey in the cupboard."

Sheriff Gabby Bloom kicked out her feet and spread out in her chair, throwing her arm over the back. "Whiskey, huh? In that case, it all started when I arrested the werewolf Loren Scandrick at Sheehan's Pub…"

The End of Book 3

CROSSING OVER EASY
Eastwind Witches Cozy Mysteries 1

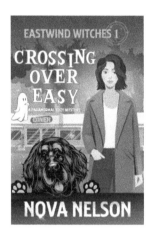

Top chef Nora Ashcroft just died. But instead of the afterlife, she's entered the magical town of Eastwind.

With a snarky hellhound familiar she doesn't want and new psychic powers she doesn't know how to use, can Nora exonerate herself from a murder by piecing together who killed the werewolf in the diner with the frying pan?

Grab a copy:
www.eastwindwitches.com/1

Get an exclusive Eastwind Witches book - free!

The Missing Motive follows a murder that takes place two years before Nora arrives in Eastwind.

With Sheriff Bloom by her side, Ruby True attempts to figure out who killed the insufferable druid who has taken up residence in her home.

Enjoy the divine duo of True and Bloom, and revisit some of your favorite Eastwind townsfolk in this humorous caper!

This book is only available to members of the Cozy Coven, Nova Nelson's reader group.

Go to www.cozycoven.com to join and claim your book!

You'll also receive updates from the town of Eastwind and gain access to games, quizzes, behind-the-scenes competitions, giveaways, and more!

About the Author

Nova Nelson grew up on a steady diet of Agatha Christie novels. She loves the mind candy of cozy mysteries and has been weaving paranormal tales since she first learned handwriting. Those two loves meet in her Eastwind Witches series, and it's about time, if she does say so herself.

When she's not busy writing, she enjoys long walks with her strong-willed dogs and eating breakfast for dinner.

Say hello:
nova@novanelson.com

CPSIA information can be obtained
at www.ICGtesting.com
Printed in the USA
LVHW092144020322
712506LV00017B/164

9 781736 728925